TONIGHT
YOU'RE
Mine

TONIGHT YOU'RE MINE

KAYLEY LORING

FUNNY SEXY SWEET ROMANCE

To those eyes and those lips and that hair and those hands…

"Love is an angel disguised as lust
Here in our bed until the morning comes"

~ Patti Smith & Bruce Springsteen, "Because the Night"

THAT NIGHT

CHAPTER 1
CHASE

There's something inherently optimistic about walking into a bar on a Friday night. It could be the beginning of a bad joke or the beginning of the rest of your life, but it's always the start of something. No matter how many bad choices you've made in a bar in the past, the future always holds the possibility of better music, just the right number of drinks, and finding the one person who just might matter more to you than anyone else.

It's the middle of spring and Brooklyn looks so fucking beautiful but I've been declining every invitation so I can stay late at the office to work. I've had zero fun and given zero fucks about anything other than keeping our startup in the black. Keaton practically begged me to meet him for a drink. He had dinner with his parents tonight and he always needs a drink after seeing his parents. He's late for meeting me, as always, but I'm glad I'm here. It's been a while.

Bitters is my favorite bar, mainly because they stock

my favorite Irish whiskey. It's pretty busy, even for nine on a Friday night. They've got strings of warm white lights hanging from the ceiling, and I don't know what it is about them that makes me want to be in love, but I've suddenly got that yearning. A quick scan of the crowd presents a few promising options, but no one who grabs my attention.

"McKay! Where ya been, man?" Denny the bartender holds his hands up in the air and greets me like a long-lost friend. We *are* old friends, actually, I've known him since we were kids.

"The office, mostly." We half-ass a bro-hug over the counter.

"Mr. Bigshot CEO over here."

"Not as glamorous as it sounds, believe me. How's your dad doin'?"

"He's all better. It was just the flu, he got over it. The usual?"

"Give it to me."

I take a seat at the bar. I had spent so many hours at this counter, dreaming up my business. With my whiskey, my notebook, and sometimes Keaton. Now that the company's a reality, and the owner of this bar is a client, all I can think about when I sit here is that I should be back at the office. As soon as Denny slides that tumbler of Redbreast in front of me, though, I'm game. I reach for my wallet, but he insists it's on the house. One of the perks of providing a service for local businesses—everything's free.

That first sip is always the best, and I revel in it, eyes closed, before turning to face the door.

I'm still feeling the glorious burn down my throat and into my chest when that door opens, and the warmth in my chest spreads everywhere. Warmth and satisfaction and a gentle ache for more. But it's not the whiskey that's making me feel this way, it's a face. It's the face that I can't look away from. Open and friendly and inquisitive and surrounded by the most luxurious dark hair that makes me want to reach all the way across the room to run my fingers through it. We're both tall enough that I can see her over the shoulders of the people standing in between us. Her eyes stay locked on mine as soon as she sees me too. She isn't smiling and she isn't frowning, but she's really looking at me.

She's nothing like the women I usually go for, and everything like the woman I could see myself coming home to every night.

She starts walking right towards me, determined but a little hesitant, like she's heading for a train that she needs to catch but she isn't quite sure if it's the right one. She's no ingénue, but there's something so pure and graceful about her expression and the way she moves. It's captivating.

It isn't until she stops in front of me that I realize the full extent of her … *everything*.

The pencil skirt, the knee-high boots, the tight sweater under the trench coat that doesn't hide her curves. The subtle swirl of fragrance—like walking past a florist shop where someone's burning incense and drinking a Hot Toddy.

Who is this woman?

I want her.

I want everything with this woman.

Her eyes are hypnotic. With the same combination of white and the warmest shade of blue, they remind me of my mom's collection of Italian pottery. Like those ceramics that I grew up with, she is beautiful in the way that everyday things are beautiful. While she doesn't look at all dainty or fragile, I find myself wanting to be extra careful with her. This is special. Somehow, already, this says "home" to me.

All she says is: "Hi there." It's the voice and direct-ness of a woman who's been to business school. I recog-nize it instantly.

"Hi."

"Who *are* you?"

"I'm Chase McKay." I hold out my hand to her. "Who are *you*?"

"Aimee Gilpin. Nice to meet you." I can hear her crystal clear over the Beastie Boys, which is impressive in a noisy bar. She's just as smooth and soft and warm as she looks, and I don't want to let go of her. We just stare at each other like we're trying to figure out if we've seen each other before. I know I haven't, because I would have remembered. "Hi," she says again. She giggles as she pats my hand, releasing herself from my grasp.

"Can I buy you a drink, Aimee Gilpin?"

"Oh, sure! Thanks. I'll have whatever you're having." So friendly. If I had to guess, I'd say she's either from Canada or the Midwest.

"You like Irish whiskey?"

"I don't know. Guess I'll find out."

I laugh. "I like your attitude." I signal to Denny that I want another glass of what I'm having. He nods, but he's busy chatting up some hipster chick.

"Is Irish whiskey your favorite drink?" She manages to ask it without sounding like she's grilling me in the way that some women do on first dates.

"I drink Scotch at home and Irish when I'm out."

"Interesting. Why is that?"

"You'll see. Irish is friendlier."

"And are you Irish or Scotch, Chase McKay?"

Oh Christ. She's got a dimple. I'm dead.

"Half Irish, half Italian."

"All trouble?" She cocks an eyebrow and smirks.

I get that a lot. I've got the shoulder-length hair, the tattoos and the beat-up old leather biker jacket, but that's just the way I look. It's not who I am. "Looks can be deceiving, Aimee."

She studies my face and says earnestly: "I believe that." She finally looks away from me to scan the room. "I like this place. I've never been here before."

"Meeting someone?"

"Yeah, my roommate. She's coming from a restaurant in the East Village. You come here often?" She asks that like she really wants to know, like she has no idea it's a line people have used forever.

"I used to. Been working a little too hard lately."

"Me too. That's why my friend basically blackmailed me into coming out tonight." She studies my face again, takes a breath, and suddenly this avalanche of words tumbles out. "I just moved out here from Michigan a few months ago," she says. "For a job.

Roxy's been my best friend since college, in Ann Arbor. She moved out here right after she graduated, but I decided to build up my resume before coming to New York. I'm glad I did. Moving here is risky, you know, but it's something I've wanted to do since I was a kid, so I needed to know that I wouldn't blow it. The last thing I wanted to do was show up in the Big Apple and get the crap kicked out of me and then have to go back home, all bitter and depressed for the rest of my life. I think it's more important to be shrewd than ballsy. Although, the ballsy people have all the fun. Are you from around here?"

I finally take a breath, even though she's the one who really needs to. "Born and raised in Brooklyn. But I know exactly what you mean. And I think you did the right thing."

Denny finally shows up to pour two fingers of whiskey in each of our tumblers, then disappears.

"Here's hoping," Aimee Gilpin says, as she raises her glass to me.

"Welcome to New York," I say, and we clink glasses. I notice her hand is trembling and it's clear to me that she's more nervous than she's letting on. Before I can tell her what to expect, she takes a big gulp.

One second after swallowing, she sticks her tongue all the way out and makes an adorable, hilarious face while stretching the fingers of her free hand out wide. Then she slams the glass down on the counter and covers her mouth.

"Guess you don't like Irish whiskey," I say.

"I am so horrified!" she says, her voice muffled.

"That bad?"

"No—well, I didn't expect it to be so sweet. But I just …" She shakes her head and waves her hand in front of her face, like she's trying to erase what just happened. "Last week I was watching this YouTube video about face yoga exercises. This woman was making all these crazy facial expressions that supposedly relax your face and get rid of wrinkles and release tension—but I was like—I would never in a million years do those exercises because if anyone ever saw me doing them, I would die of embarrassment. And I just made one of those faces. In a bar. In front of you. So that's awesome."

I lean in towards her and say: "Guess we'll have to find another way for you to release tension."

She laughs, nervously, and then stops to look at me. "You know what? It has a really nice aftertaste." And then she realizes the subtext of my comment about releasing tension, and her cheeks turn the most amazing shade of deep pink. "Oh my," she exhales.

'Oh my.' Who says that?

The song changes to a quiet ballad, a Jackson Browne song that my mom loves. The sudden shift from thumping bass to soulful piano changes the air around us and the molecules inside of everyone in here, and the awareness shifts from the lower torso up to the heart. I fucking love the playlists in this bar, and I fucking love the way this woman is looking at me like I'm some deep philosophical question that she doesn't know the answer to but she's willing to muddle through anyway.

"Try it again," I say, nodding towards her glass. "Take a sip and close your eyes. It's meant to be savored."

Slowly lifting that tumbler to her beautiful lips, she takes a sip and closes those gorgeous eyes of hers—sky blue and black. I savor her like my whiskey, so jealous of the rim of the glass that gets to touch her lips. I watch her respond to every smooth and warm, surprising flavor as it caresses her tongue—the fruity honeyed sweetness, the sherry and licorice and ginger, the peppery spice that erupts in her throat as she swallows, the hint of toffee that lingers. When she opens her eyes again and looks at me, she lets out a sigh, and I know that she gets it now. The union and explosion of unexpected soulmate flavors that can change the way you experience the world. It's like drinking music. Just a taste and you know how big and magical and soft this dangerous collision of contradictions can be.

But two seconds later, she shakes herself out of the reverie and I can see her trying to rein in her fear of that big magic. I get it. She doesn't know if she can handle it. Then her expression changes again and I get the feeling she's about to surprise both of us.

"So, I don't usually do this, but … here's my number." She hands me a folded-up piece of notepaper that already has her name and number written on it. "My roommate dared me to give a guy that I like my number even if he doesn't ask me for it. So just in case there's a hurricane or a zombie apocalypse in the next hour or so, I'll get this out of the way now."

"Thank you. I would have asked you for your number anyway."

"Well, that's nice to know."

I reach for a napkin on the bar and pull out the pen from my pocket.

"I don't usually give beautiful women who don't like whiskey my number, but in case of hurricane or zombie apocalypse … This is my cell phone, if you need assistance." I hand her the napkin with my name and number on it.

"I appreciate it. I keep a pretty cool head during natural disasters, but I lie awake at night worrying about zombies." She carefully folds up the napkin and places it in her purse.

"I can definitely help you get to sleep if necessary."

I take off my leather jacket, expose the ink, so she knows it's not just a long-hair situation she'd have to deal with.

Her eyes widen as they scan the parts of my arms that aren't hidden by my T-shirt. I can tell she likes what she sees, but she gets a whiff of something that she does not like when I move my jacket to my lap.

"Do you smoke?"

"Not much anymore. I used to … up until an hour ago."

"You really shouldn't smoke."

"I have been meaning to quit."

"You really should." Her spine straightens and she places her glass down on the bar again and actually raises her index finger in front of my face and wags it. "Smoking damages nearly every organ in your body, you know, not just your lungs. And not just your organs—your brain and your bones and your cardiovascular system! It's shortening your lifespan by more than a decade. There's poison in tobacco you know. It's not just the nicotine, you're inhaling carbon monoxide and tar! I just don't know why anyone would do that to themselves —not to mention the people around them. And cancer— do you want to talk about cancer, Chase McKay?"

"I really don't."

I think I just quit smoking.

"Point taken. You got some sort of rule about *not* kissing smokers, Aimee?"

The lighting in here may be dim, but I can see her blushing even harder. She clears her throat. "I did … up until a minute ago."

I think I just quit other women.

When I sit up straight on this barstool, Aimee and I are about the same height. She's staring at my mouth and her lips are parted. I'm not aware of how much time has passed since she walked in here, but I've been wanting to kiss her for what feels like forever. Leaning towards her, I notice her chest expanding as she prepares herself for my kiss. Just when she starts to lean in towards me too, a hand slaps her on the shoulder.

"Aim! Honey! I am so fucking sorry I'm late! That fucking F train has it in for me, I swear."

The woman whips her around for a hug while giving me the once-over.

I can't tell if Aimee is frustrated or relieved by the interruption—maybe both. Maybe I'm feeling the same way too. Her friend sizes-up the situation. I can't tell if she's impressed or amused or both.

"Well, fuck me," she mutters.

"Uh, Roxy, this is Chase. Chase—Roxy."

"Hello there, Chase."

Shaking Roxy's hand, I utter a friendly "Hey, how are you?" but I turn my attention right back to Aimee. I can tell that Aimee's probably used to men gawking at her friend, and I just won a few points for not being most men. But Aimee is not most women. Not to me. Not tonight.

"I was just encouraging Chase here to quit smoking."

"Is *that* what you were doing? Can I just borrow Aimee for one second?" She pulls Aimee a couple of feet away and yells in her ear.

I, along with the whole bar, can hear Roxy tell her: "You need to take it down a notch, Professor McGonagall."

"What?!"

"I saw the way you were lecturing him when I walked in. You might as well just flash him your granny panties."

"What?! No, I'm being a sexy teacher."

"No. You're not."

Yeah. She is, Roxy. She is.

Then I overhear Roxy utter the word "bet" before Aimee shushes her with a murderous look. Roxy walks off to join a group of people she knows, without another word. Aimee watches her walk away before removing her coat and draping it over the barstool next to me.

"Sorry about that," she says.

I can see the outline of a black bra beneath her tight creamy white sweater and I'm pretty sure I'd forgive her for absolutely anything.

"Sorry about lecturing you." She stares at her hands. "It's none of my business, I just think you're great and I want you to live, and not have to breathe through a hole in your throat."

"You don't have to apologize. And thanks."

She looks over at me and pouts.

We both laugh.

"Can I get you another drink?"

"Yes! Dear God, yes!" The voice belongs to my best friend Keaton. I had completely forgotten that I was here waiting for him. Aimee is quite the distraction. She may be the distraction I've been waiting for my whole life.

"You would not believe the night I've had," he continues, shaking his head. "You don't know how lucky you are to have the parents you have, man." He really does look beaten down. As beaten down as a guy can look in a bespoke suit and coat and shoes that cost more than my rent. And then he notices Aimee, and the outline of that black bra beneath her tight creamy white sweater. "And I cannot believe how much better my night just got. Hello there." He holds his hand out. Instead of shaking Aimee's hand, he places his other hand over it and just stares at her.

Fucking hell.

"This is Aimee. I was just asking if I can get *her* another drink."

"Aimee," he says. "I'm Keaton Bridges. Hi." I know that tone of voice. Every time Keaton switches to that golden tone of voice, he has gone home with the woman on the receiving end of it. I've got that sinking feeling and my whole body clenches up. If I didn't love him so much, I'd already have kicked his teeth in by now.

He doesn't even realize he's cockblocking me, because it just wouldn't occur to him that he and I would want the same thing. It rarely happens. We both wanted to go to Wharton. We both wanted to start my business. One of us did both of those things by studying and working his ass off, and one of us had the money to do whatever the fuck he wanted.

I watch how Aimee responds to Keaton's immediate full-court press. She's so nice and polite. It's hard to tell at first if she's being friendly with the best friend, like I was with Roxy, or if she's falling for this shit.

"Why don't *I* get you a drink." Keaton is really laying it on thick. "What have you got there?" He sees the tumbler behind her on the counter and grimaces. "Do *not* tell me he made you drink Irish whiskey? That stuff is nasty."

"I think I'm acquiring a taste for it, actually," she says.

"Admirable, but I bet you're more of a...Moscow Mule kind of girl."

She twists her lips to the side and glances over at me apologetically. "I do love Moscow Mules."

"Denny!" Keaton leans in against the bar, right between me and Aimee. "Two Moscow Mules and another whiskey for my friend here." He stays in place between me and Aimee and says, "Damn, Aimee. You smell incredible. That's Chanel, isn't it?"

"It is. You've got a good nose!"

What follows is the kind of conversation that only Keaton can have with a woman. About his grandmother being friends with Coco Chanel. It might be true and it might be total horseshit, but he sells it like the best car salesman. I know this guy so well. I know when he's making an effort with a woman and when he's on auto-pilot, and he's actually making an effort with Aimee. I can see, out of the corner of my eye, that Aimee is trying to maneuver herself so she can include me in the conversation, but it's no use. Everything's fading away and I'm retreating inside where I can have a tactical meeting with myself in my board room.

Thank God I went to business and law school. I've learned how to make rational, informed decisions. My heart's telling me this is a woman worth fighting for, but my brain's telling me that's not my heart talking. It's my dick. It's the whiskey. It's the strings of warm white lights. It's the Jackson fucking Browne song.

It's not that she isn't worth fighting for. It's that I have to pick my battles. And I am not going to pick a battle with my best friend and business partner. Not now, anyway.

I've known Keaton for nearly a decade. He let me live in his apartment in Philadelphia for four years when we were at Wharton and nearly kicked me out once when he was convinced that his girlfriend was in love with me. She wasn't. He didn't. We got through it. I founded a company with him less than two years ago —a company that he invested the seed money for, and I need him on my side when we're voting at a board meeting soon. I've known Aimee for less than half an hour and had one drink with her. If she doesn't want to kiss a guy who smokes, then she won't be kissing a guy who smokes. Not tonight, anyway. Even though I never want to see another cigarette again in my life.

Just because I've never experienced love at first sight before, it doesn't mean it'll never happen again. I see how this is going to go and I need to leave sooner rather than later, so I don't end up in a pissing contest.

I swallow the whiskey that Keaton ordered for me, stand up and put my jacket back on. I shake Aimee's hand and say, "It was a pleasure meeting you. Enjoy your Moscow Mule." The look on her pretty face could break my heart if I'd let it. But I won't let it.

I pat Keaton on the back and tell him I'm heading back to the office. He barely protests. He doesn't want to lose Aimee's focus. I don't blame him. I didn't either. But I will.

The road to a successful business is littered with sacrifices, and Aimee may not be the first, but she is certainly my favorite thing that I'll be letting go of to make this business work.

And so, I've heard some good music and had just the right number of drinks and met a woman who could have mattered to me more than anyone—in another life. I've made a choice, and it might be a bad choice, but it's the right one.

I walk back out into the surprisingly cold night, but I'm not alone. You're never alone at night in New York, and Brooklyn is still so fucking beautiful. I feel a chill, but it's got nothing to do with the temperature. It's knowing that if I turned around and looked back through that door that I just walked out of, I'd see Aimee watching me. If I stayed there looking back at her long enough, she'd follow me outside and leave Keaton behind. I know it deep in my lungs and all my organs and my brain and my bones and my cardiovascular system, just as well as I know that I'm going to keep walking away, even though I'll be thinking about those deep blue eyes long after I close mine tonight.

TONIGHT

CHAPTER 2
AIMEE

ONE MONTH LATER

I've been wearing yoga pants all day, because I was hoping it would make me feel more Zen about everything, but it turns out it's not that easy to feel Zen when you're frantically stuffing your face with donuts. It's just so disappointing that no matter how delicious and comforting they are, they all start to taste the same after your third or fourth or fifth. No matter how much icing or sprinkles or filling, they're still so simple. A quick fix. They'll never wake up your palate with breathtaking contradictory flavors and leave a smooth, complex, haunting aftertaste like certain other vices do.

This has been the longest two-day weekend ever and it's nowhere near over yet.

Also, my roommate keeps handing me bottles of

beer and taking them away when I've finished so I can't keep track of how many I've had. Beer and donuts are a terrible combination, but also strangely appropriate for the occasion. I lick the melted chocolate icing from my thumb and call out: "Roxy! How many beers have I had?!"

"If you're sober enough to ask without slurring, it's not enough!" she calls out, from the bathroom. I can tell from her voice that she's curling her eyelashes. She has Make-Up Face voice. She's listening to Prince. That means she's getting ready to go out, which means she's getting ready to convince *me* to go out. I do appreciate that she stayed in with me on Friday and Saturday night, *but* …

"I start a new job tomorrow!"

"Exactly! We're celebrating. And you need to drink one beer for every month that you've been celibate."

"I am not going to drink six bottles of beer on a Sunday night, Roxy."

"Fine. Then one beer for every week you wasted being polite to that bonehead."

"I'm not going to drink four beers either. I'm serious! How many have I had?"

"Three, sweetie. Only three."

I exhale and then polish off my third bottle of beer.

"He's not a bonehead," I say meekly.

He really isn't.

Keaton is good-looking and he looks amazing in a suit. Keaton is charming, in the way that eight-year-old boys are charming. A good guy. But not the guy for me.

When he showed up at the bar that first night that I

met him and Chase, I had the exact opposite response to him as I did to his best friend. When I saw Chase, my body immediately went on high alert. I assumed he was the lead singer of some grunge band that I wasn't cool enough to recognize, but I could totally see myself screaming up at him from a mosh pit, begging for his attention. When he saw me and held my gaze, I just kept walking toward him. I've never done that before in my life—walked up to some stranger in a bar and started talking? He made me feel like some heightened version of myself, like an awesome drug that I'd probably never try. I was turned on. Actually switched on, like a lightbulb that had been set to dim forever and then BAM! *Here's all that electricity we've been holding back from you! How do you like that?!* It felt like the difference between walking around your hometown and walking around Manhattan for the first time. Suddenly you're so aware and awake and anything could happen.

I liked it and I was afraid of it.

When Keaton showed up, he felt familiar and safe. It was like getting off a roller coaster. I still had the dizzying buzz from flirting with Chase, but I was stepping back onto solid ground again and needing to find my balance. But it's not like I didn't want to get back on that roller coaster! If I were put in a situation where I had to make a choice, I would have chosen Chase. But he took himself out of the equation.

It's not that I wasn't flattered by Keaton's attention.

He's like a purebred puppy who doesn't understand the word "no." He's exasperating, but you can't hate him because at the end of the day, he's still a cute puppy. And I'm too old to date puppies.

Which is why I would have rather dated Chase. The day after meeting him, I sent a text to the number he'd given me.

It was great meeting you and Irish whiskey at Bitters last night! Haven't seen any zombies yet, but you never know...

Cute, right?

No response.

Ever.

I mean. Maybe he gave me a wrong number. But I had a feeling it was a Bro Code thing. I get it. I don't like it, but I get it.

A few days later, I had a phone conversation with Keaton and I learned more about their relationship, so I could certainly see why Chase didn't want to rock the boat.

I liked Keaton. I really did. I especially liked that he had such a cool best friend. But I also hated that he was friends with Chase. Because I *really* liked Chase.

But I'm a nice, polite Midwesterner, and Keaton is persistent. Every few days he'd call or text to invite me out to all these great restaurants. And all the flowers he sent to my office? Oh lord, so many beautiful flowers. And *Wicked*. He said he could get us greats seats at *Wicked* on Broadway. Roxy and I always used to sing

"Defying Gravity" when we were drunk at karaoke bars in college. That was a tough one to say 'no' to, but I did.

And then I found out that I was being laid off. The job that I had moved out here for—at the prestigious business consulting firm—had to eliminate my position. So I had a lot more on my mind than dating.

The next few times he asked me out, I gave him the excuse of being stressed-out from job-hunting. On Thursday, I found him waiting for me outside my apartment when I came home from a job interview. He had a lunch reservation at a great restaurant by the river and wanted me to go with him right then. He was very charming and persuasive, but I just couldn't go out with him if there was ever a chance that I could be with Chase. I didn't tell him that, of course. What I finally told him, very clearly, was that I liked him but I didn't think we were a good match and I really didn't want to lead him on. He seemed to think I was joking at first. I'm guessing no one's ever said those words to him before.

For a few seconds, I saw this storm of indignant anger in his eyes, and I understood why Chase didn't want to take any chances. But as quickly as that look in his eyes appeared, it was replaced by polite words of thanks, a sincere handshake, and a genuine "Good luck with everything. Let's keep in touch. I hope to see you again sometime."

He was classy. I felt good about everything. I wondered if and when he'd mention to his best friend that I'd totally refused to date him. I wondered how long I should wait before "accidentally" running into Chase in the neighborhood after subtly and ever-so elegantly stalking him.

That was Thursday. That was before shit got weird.

"Lady, lady, lady …" my roommate says as she collapses onto the sofa next to me. She's got her going-out face on, she's got her I'm-getting-laid-tonight musk on, and I can't help but laugh. Roxy looks like Betty from the *Archie* comics, if Betty were drawn by a horny twelve-year-old boy who's into manga. Blonde pony-tail, pert nose, comically enormous boobs that are packed tight into a 1950's teen-girl outfit, and a sweet smile that does nothing to hide the foul-mouthed vixen's devious thoughts. She takes the empty donut box from me and says, "You finally got another fucking job. It's a good thing. We should be celebrating."

That's right. On Friday afternoon, I got a call from Elaine Hoffman. Elaine is the president of the boutique business consulting firm that I interviewed with on Thursday. I had been unemployed for nearly three weeks. I was deliriously happy when she offered me a position at her firm, because her company specializes in consulting for startups, and that was my focus in business school. The pay is great, the office is in Brooklyn, I loved her no-bullshit attitude and I just knew we'd be a great fit. And then she told me that the project she's assigning me to, starting Monday, is for her important new clients: SnapLegal-NYC. Keaton and Chase's company. They hired her company and they're paying for an on-site project manager for a month. She hired me *specifically* because she needs a project manager to help them transition to a subscription-based model for their services, although she never mentioned this in our meeting. "You're a Godsend," she said. "You're a perfect fit for this."

That means I get to see Chase McKay on Monday! I thought to myself. *I wonder if he wears suits at the office?* I thought to myself, before imagining him slowly taking off his suit.

It wasn't until after I'd hung up that I realized I'd also be seeing Keaton Bridges on Monday.

I immediately called Roxy at work, and told her about my situation. She laughed so hard she didn't even make a sound, then she snorted, then she hung up on me. The fifteen random emojis she sent afterwards made no sense and didn't make me feel any better.

I drank one cup of coffee spiked with just a tiny amount of Irish whiskey and a huge amount of cream, and I called Elaine back.

"I just had my HR woman send a courier over with your paperwork and a company cell phone," she said when she answered. "Please don't tell me you've changed your mind."

"I haven't changed my mind about working for you, Elaine, not at all. I just have a bit of a dilemma here, and I felt that I should tell you that I actually know the founders of SnapLegal, a little bit. I met them socially, and Keaton Bridges pursued me for a few weeks, but I finally made it clear to him that I wouldn't go out with him. He was always a perfect gentleman and it was a friendly parting. No hard or deep feelings at all, and I promise you that I am fully capable of doing the job your company has been hired to do for them. I just … you know … full-disclosure."

"And what about Chase McKay?"

"What about him?"

Oh shit. Did I accidentally verbalize my little Chase McKay in a suit fantasy without knowing it? Did I think those dirty thoughts so loud that my new boss could hear them?

"You said that you know the founders socially." I could hear the strain in her voice. She was trying so hard not to yell at me. "Did Chase McKay also pursue you?"

"Oh God, no! No no nooooo." *I wish.* "No, I just know him because he's Keaton's best friend. I mean, I actually met him half an hour before I met Keaton, but that was it." *And I overanalyzed his reasons for not wanting to pursue me endlessly.*

I heard her exhale slowly. "Okay. So that's your big dilemma? You dated Keaton Bridges a few times, and now you are not dating him, but it's a friendly break-up?"

"Yes. I mean, no! It wasn't even a break-up because we never dated. We're just not dating. End of story."

"Okay. Here's a short story for you: I once had to work for the man who ran over my dog. I wanted to murder him, but I did my job because I am a professional who is capable of compartmentalizing. That is why I did not spit in his coffee once, as far as he knew."

"I'm … so sorry about your dog."

"Okay." I could hear her tapping on her desk with her pen. "Listen. I have three kids and I am currently the main breadwinner in my family because my husband has decided that it's finally time for him to write The Great American Novel, and I haven't slept for more than four hours a night in months, so I don't have time to filter my thoughts on this and then get back to you. I like you. I had a good feeling about you. You have the perfect resume for this position and fantastic references. And you are literally, on paper, the best person for this SnapLegal job. So, if you are honestly telling me that your personal dynamic with our clients will not affect your ability to do your best work and represent my company in a professional manner, then I seriously don't give a shit about your private life, as long as you keep it private. So just sign and return the contract. Your company e-mail address will be set up by Monday morning, and I will meet you at the SnapLegal offices at ten on Monday morning for a quick meeting with the founders. But if they try to get out of my contract with them because of *you*, then obviously I will be firing you."

She hung up before I could thank her for under-standing. I also sort of wanted to ask her to marry me. If she was cool about the situation, now all I had to do was make sure that Keaton would be cool with it. And I was nearly positive that he probably would be. I just wished there was one person that I could talk to about how to approach this, someone who knows Keaton better than I do, someone with impossibly beautiful wavy hair and rich, dark bedroom eyes and a deep smooth voice that always sounds like he's talking dirty on the phone—even when he's grumbling to you about Moscow Mules and walking away from you.

"I need to talk to Chase," I say, reaching for my phone. I've already called him twice and texted him three times today.

"Has he responded?"

I sigh. "No."

"Send him a boob pic."

I bark out a laugh. "That's your answer to every man problem."

"That's *the* answer to every man problem. You can send him one of mine if you'd like." She smiles big and bats her eyelashes at me.

She's joking. She's never actually taken or sent boob pics. It's a joke. I'm pretty sure it's a joke.

Roxy is an angel. She's an angel disguised as the little blonde devil perched on my shoulder. The one who convinces me that a shot or three of tequila and going dancing are the answer to all of my problems. And they were! When we were in college.

Roxy works just as hard as she plays. She's the manager of customer loyalty for an online retail company, and she makes a buttload of money, some of which she has been using to pay for most of our meals for the past few weeks. I am eternally grateful to her. Except for one thing.

"This is all your fault. If you hadn't bet me that I

couldn't give a guy my number, I wouldn't have gone out that night and maybe I would have met Chase another time, when Keaton wasn't around."

I had only been out on a few dates since moving to New York, because I seem to be really good at attracting guys that I'm *not* really attracted to. Roxy dared me to go home with a guy that I met in a bar. When I refused to acknowledge that one, she dared me to give my number to a guy that I actually liked and to give a fake number to any guy I didn't like if he asked me for one. That was the one and only time I had ever actually taken her advice ...Well, sort of ... Minus the fake number part.

I can't *not* stay in touch with people. I still send Christmas cards to my friends from kindergarten. I send thank you cards to former bosses when I've been laid off. Every stationary store in New York is still in business because of me.

But I couldn't give Keaton a fake number, because I didn't want him to tell Chase that I was a sneaky b-face.

She brushes the hair out of my eyes. "If you want Chase, go get him."

"I can't *get* Chase. I have to go to work *with* Chase *and* Keaton tomorrow."

"Why don't you just ask your new boss to assign you to a different project?"

"She specifically hired me because she needs someone on this one."

"Then quit. You'll get another job."

"Wow. You are full of great ideas. Maybe I should also do heroin while I'm at it."

"Hey, don't knock it until you try it."

"That's not funny."

"Sorry. Don't do heroin. But you should definitely do Chase. I mean, the man quit smoking for you."

"He did not quit smoking for me."

"You said he quit smoking."

"Keaton mentioned that he did, when we were on the phone."

"Right after he met you and you criticized him for smoking."

"I'm quite sure I'm not the only one who's ever criticized him for smoking. He obviously hates me, or he wouldn't have bolted from the bar like it was on fire."

"Maybe he's secretly burning for you." She grins and waggles her perfect eyebrows. "Call him again."

"I've already texted him three times to tell him that I really need to talk to him and called twice. He probably thinks I'm a stalker now."

"Did you leave a voicemail?"

"Nobody leaves voicemails."

"Do you know where he lives?"

"Not exactly."

I just want to tell Chase that I have a new job at the consulting firm that they hired for implementation consultation and that I've been assigned to their project. I just want to make sure he's okay with it and discuss how best to approach this with Keaton. I want to have this conversation with him, because I need this job and I'm a professional and he's a professional and we're all grown-ups. Also, I want to hear his voice and smell him just a little.

"I think I might know where Chase is…" I say, hesitantly.

"In your dirty dreams every night?"

"At that bar in Carroll Gardens."

Roxy claps her hands so loud that it echoes around the room. "Yes! That is where you need to go. That is what you need to do. And I know exactly what you need to wear when you go there to do that."

"But it's seven o'clock. On a Sunday. I start a new job in the morning."

"Yeah! Woohoo!"

"But I mean … we're *twenty-seven* years old."

"Girl. Do not make me slap you."

CHAPTER 3
CHASE

There's something pathetic about walking into a bar at seven-thirty on a Sunday night. Why would anyone go out alone to drink on a Sunday night unless they were trying to avoid something or someone that they don't want to deal with? That's avoiding your current problems by creating future problems. And what kind of idiot returns to the scene of the crime to try to forget about the thief of his heart?

This kind of idiot, apparently.

I powered off my phone as soon as I got home from the gym. Removed the SIM card and put it in an envelope in a drawer. Now I'm at Bitters, handing over my phone to Denny so he can put it in the safe in the back office. I'm giving him fifty bucks to keep the Irish whiskey coming and an order to not give the phone back to me tonight—no matter what. No matter how drunk I get, no matter how much I beg and plead with him to give me my phone so I can call the girl who just shot down my best friend, he must not let me have it.

I may look and fuck like a bad boy, but I've done the right thing my whole life, because I couldn't afford not to. Not when I was a kid and my parents were working their asses off at the restaurant every day and night. Not when I was in high school when I realized being successful meant being smarter and working ten times harder than the entitled rich guys who were invading Brooklyn. Not at Wharton or law school when I realized the aforementioned situation would never change, even though the snobby girlfriends of those entitled rich guys secretly eye-fucked me while smoothing down their cashmere sweater sets. And not even now that I'm at a point in my life where I'm starting to wonder— what's the point of being successful if I don't have a woman I love to share that success with?

Tonight, I'm going to keep doing the right thing, no matter what. For the sake of my friendship with Keaton. For the sake of my company and my partnership with Keaton. For the sake of everything I've worked for up until now. No matter how much it's killing me.

"What would you say to that girl if you allowed yourself to talk to her now?" Denny asks, as he pours out three more fingers of the good stuff.

"Don't be a bartender shrink with me, man," I say as I'm hunched over the bar like a guy who's desperate for a bartender shrink.

"We're just talking. It's slow tonight, come on. Indulge me."

"I'm not gonna talk to her."

"Hypothetically. If she walked in here right now?"

Fortunately, a few ladies come up to order, so I'm spared the humiliation of pouring out my soul to a bartender. I've never done it before and I'm not going to start now. But what would I say to her?

Love was the last thing on my mind until I walked into this bar that night. All I cared about at that point in my life was getting my business to thrive. I've never fallen in love at first sight before or since, but I felt it when I saw you walk in here. You looked nothing like the women I usually go for, but I couldn't look away. I could tell you weren't the kind of woman who needed to be stared at, and I could tell I wasn't your type of guy, but I just wanted to know you. And when you walked right up to me it felt like everyone and everything around us was dimming and fading out.

Every word out of your mouth—and there were so many of them—made me want to kiss you. I should have just kissed you. I should have stayed after Keaton showed up. I should have fought for you. But Keaton and I were partners in a new business that was less than two years old, a business that I'd spent years planning and that he invested his own money in. I couldn't risk taking a stand that night if Keaton really liked you too, and I could tell that he did. I couldn't blame him for that.

I tell that guy when he's being an idiot or an asshole all day long every day, but getting between Keaton and a woman that he likes is never a good idea.

I'm sorry I never responded to your text the next day. I had already heard from Keaton that he got your number. I figured I'd hold off and see if it went anywhere for you guys or not. My money was on 'not.' I didn't expect him to keep pursuing you for so long, but he thought you were just playing hard to get.

I don't usually have regrets. I'm usually a lot better at moving on. I've passed on job offers from Fortune 500 companies. I've turned down generous investors because I didn't like their politics. There are ten million women in New York, and all of a sudden, I was hung up on one of them.

For that first week after I walked away from you, I was so fucking messed up I was listening to Coldplay. Coldplay, Aimee.

And then I forced myself to accept the consequences of my choice. Every time Keaton told me about how sweet and great you were on the phone, I died a little inside. I tried to hate you for not being direct with him right from the start, but I couldn't. I only hated myself for not being more assertive with him and I couldn't believe he was blowing it even after I'd taken myself out of the equation. I was glad he was bombing with you, but honestly, at least it would have been worth the sacrifice if he ended up with you. I know Keaton, and if he likes you but he can't have you, you will still be off-limits for me, for life.

I managed to stop picturing you in bed with my best friend. I almost stopped imagining you in bed with me. I convinced myself that you were all wrong for me, and maybe you are. I convinced myself that I'd meet someone I like more than you, and maybe I still will. But I can't seem to fall out of love with what could have been.

This has been the longest month ever.

I finally quit smoking because of you, so I've been in a shit mood for two reasons.

A couple of weeks ago, I was inside a coffee shop on Court Street and I looked out and saw you alone on your Schwinn bicycle with a basket on the handlebars, probably going to the market. I thought of my favorite Jimi Hendrix song "Little Wing," because you looked all butterflies and zebras and moonbeams and fairytales, riding with the wind. You stopped to talk to someone who was walking her puppy, and you were so friendly and happy and cute with that dog. I told myself I'd count to ten slowly and if you were still there by the time I was done, I'd run out to you and tell you how I felt because — fuck it all — at least you'd know. But you were pedaling away before I got to seven, and there wasn't enough coffee in the world to get me out of the funk I fell into for the rest of that day.

I've been listening to the blues ever since Keaton told me what you said to him. I encouraged him to go out and hook up with someone else. He never stopped seeing other women. To be honest, he met a socialite named Quinn soon after he met you. But she wouldn't sleep with him unless they were exclusive and he liked you enough to see if it would go anywhere with you. Now he's off in the Hamptons with her.

I've been fighting the urge to call you and let you know how much I want you, just to avoid a fight with Keaton.

I spent three hours at the gym, yesterday and today, to keep myself busy and tire myself out. I still can't stop thinking about you, but I have to.

So tonight, I'm going to force myself to go home with someone else, and this whiskey is going to get me there. Because that's what it's going to take to keep me from trying to find you tonight. Even though I never did stop seeing your deep blue eyes when I shut mine at night. Even though, without wanting to, I still look for you everywhere.

"Having a good night?" a sultry voice asks, as I'm overwhelmed by perfume. Big curly hair. Big grin. Big everything. That fucking Chainsmokers song comes on and everyone in this place starts nodding their head and singing along. Sure. This will do. For tonight. It's not what I want, but it will have to do.

CHAPTER 4
AIMEE

Roxy has to physically push me the last half a block to Bitters. She made me wear a camisole under the blouse that had shrunk a full size when I put it in the dryer. The one that I was going to donate to Goodwill. I can't even button it up over my boobs. I might as well be wearing a flashing neon necklace that points down to my cleavage. This is not the way a business consultant dresses when she wants to discuss a professional matter with a client. But Roxy reminded me that technically I'm still unemployed until midnight, which means that Chase isn't my client yet.

Bless her devious heart.

And also damn her.

She pulls my jacket off of me before opening the door. "Show those girls off and let them breathe," she says.

I let out a little laugh before trying to take a deep breath, but everything gets stuck in my chest.

• • •

When we walk in, that Chainsmokers song that Roxy and I love is just ending, and I get that rush that you feel when you hear a favorite song in public, like it's a sign that you're meant to be here right now. And then I see him, Chase, and my stomach flips and then drops. He's at that same seat at the bar where I saw him a month ago. This time, there isn't a sea of people between us, but just like the last time—he looks over to check who's walked in and as soon as he sees me, he doesn't look away.

Only this time, he's hunched over. His dark soulful eyes are so sad. Those are the eyes of a man who sits alone in a dive bar on a weekday afternoon, not an impossibly sexy young CEO who currently has a buxom brunette hanging all over him.

"Get it, girl," Roxy whispers into my ear as she rubs my back for reassurance and then dances across the room to a booth to join a guy that she knows.

Now it's just me standing by the door staring at my former pursuer's best friend, and Chase staring back at me while the buxom brunette continues to flaunt her buxomness in his face. I don't know exactly how to read his expression. Is it remorse, relief or resignation? Whatever it is, it's breaking my heart. His eyes stay fixed on me while I hesitantly walk toward him.

"Hi there," I say, lacking all of the confidence and hope that I had in my voice the first time we met.

"Hi," he says, with the voice of a man who still has whiskey burning the back of his throat.

I smile at the woman next to him, waiting for an introduction that doesn't come. She just looks back and forth from Chase to me, rolls her eyes, and pulls a pen out from her purse. She writes her name and number on a cocktail napkin and leaves it on the bar next to Chase before walking off to join her friends at a booth. Without even looking at it, Chase flips the napkin over and places his drink on top of it.

He doesn't smell like cigarettes at all anymore. He smells like hot sex in front of a fire in a log cabin in the mountains—not that I'd know what that actually smells like. He looks like he's had as anxiety-provoking a weekend as I have, minus the donuts.

"Are you okay?"

"Been better. You want a drink?"

"No. I just came here to ... Are you ... What happened? You don't have to tell me. I'm sure you don't want to ..."

He just looks at me, with a pained expression.

"Um. Okay, so I'm sure I'm the last person you want to talk to right now, but—"

"You're wrong."

"What?"

"You're wrong about that, Aimee."

Just hearing him say my name out loud makes me weak in the knees. It was a terrible idea, coming here. Or maybe the best idea I've ever had.

"Okay, well that's a good thing to be wrong about, I suppose."

He smiles, a tired smile. God, it's good to see him smile. Even that sad, exhausted smile.

Stay focused.

You came here to discuss business, not stare at his mouth.

I swear, most of the time, the voice in my head sounds like a Disney princess with an MBA. But when I'm around Chase McKay, I find myself thinking things like: *I want to grab onto that hair and ride that man like a mechanical bull*, or *I wonder what he tastes like. Everywhere.*

Good God.

What if I've had the nymphomaniac gene my whole life and it took meeting Chase McKay to activate it?

Focus.

Be professional.

"I've been wanting to touch you—I mean—I've been trying to *get in touch with you* about something. Not what you probably think …"

That sad little smile of his curls into a grin.

I touch my hand to my neck. My skin is hot. It feels like someone has set fire to my clothes. I would walk directly into an ice-cold shower right now if I could.

"I don't have my phone on me," he explains. As if that isn't cause for alarm in the twenty-first century.

"Oh no! Did you lose it?"

"No."

"Oh … okay. Well, I don't know if you've talked to Keaton at all this weekend …"

He looks down at my hands which are clasped together in front of me like … Professor McGonagall. "I have," he answers.

"Okay … is he … um … He's fine with everything, right?"

He blinks, slowly. "Sure."

"Great! I mean, I'm glad."

"He was very disappointed, though."

"Oh. Well, I'm sure he'll get over it though, right?"

"I can't speak for him."

"I know. I didn't…I don't mean to put you in this position. I mean, I certainly didn't plan to be in this position either."

"What position would you like to be in?"

My eyes widen as I suck in a breath.

All of the positions.

I want to be in all of the positions.

With you.

I remember this.

This is what it was like the night we met, before Keaton showed up.

"Maybe I will have a drink."

Chase raises his hand, without looking at the bartender, and the guy comes right over. But I can't stop staring at Chase's hand. Those long beautiful fingers that could play me like a piano.

"What can I get you?" the bartender asks me, raising his chin.

"Irish whiskey, please. Redbreast. Neat." I can feel Chase staring at me, but I can't handle looking at his face right now. "Where is Roxy?" I look around for my friend, and quickly find that she's in a booth, sitting on a guy's lap. Well, that was fast. I recognize him, though. She's been out with him a couple of times. I keep trying to send her telepathic messages to come over and talk to me, tear me away from this man before I say or do something that I really shouldn't say or do. She won't look at me. On purpose. I'm getting telepathic messages from her that are telling me to say and do the things that I really want to say and do to him. Or maybe that's just my hormones yelling at me.

The bartender slides a glass of Irish whiskey towards me. While he refills Chase's glass with the same, I reach for my wallet inside my purse.

Chase's hand, those beautiful long fingers, touch my forearm and I freeze.

"I got this," he says.

"Thank you," I whisper. I don't breathe again until he finally lets go of me. Then I take a sip of this fascinating liquid, close my eyes and savor it, in the way that I should have the first time I tried it.

Chase slams his empty glass back down on the counter, drags the back of his hand across the bottom of his lower lip and then looks me straight in the eyes. "Why did you come here tonight, Aimee?"

"I wanted to talk to you about … about …"

"Keaton?"

"Sort of."

"Did you change your mind about him? Do you want to date him now?"

"No." I suppose I should have wavered a moment before answering, but that's the truth. I don't.

I try not to stare at his mouth while he strokes the scruff on his chin with his fingers, contemplating me.

"So, what do you want to talk about?"

God, the way he's looking up at me, with those dark heavy-lidded eyes and his head tilted. One arm is leaning against the bar, the rest of his body is open to me as I stand there next to him clutching my drink and clenching my thighs together.

I take another sip of whiskey and swallow hard. "I just wanted you to know that I really liked you when we first met and I wanted to get to know you, but I think I felt intimidated by you. That's why I was talking so much and that's why I started talking to your friend when he showed up. But it was you. *You* were the one I was attracted to. I mean, I did like Keaton—he's very nice and fun—but with you it was … bigger. I understand why you backed off. I probably shouldn't have given my number to him at all, but … I wasn't sure if you were really even interested. I don't want to cause any kind of problem between you guys. That's the last thing I want to do, but I just had to say it. I just wanted you to know how I felt. How I feel." I take another sip of whiskey to stop myself from saying anything else.

I'll just make a mess of things and wait for Elaine Hoffman to fire me.

She'll be fine.

Her company will be fine.

SnapLegal will be fine.

I'll just move back to Ann Arbor and live with my parents.

I'm only twenty-seven.

I'll bounce back.

Worth it.

Right, whiskey?

Oh shit, what have I done?

. . .

Before I can excuse myself and run to grab Roxy for an emergency meeting in the ladies room, Chase says, "I came here tonight because I haven't been able to stop thinking about you."

At least I think that's what he said. I think he was talking to me, even though he's staring at his empty glass. I lower myself down a bit, to rest my elbows on the bar top. My ear is now closer to Chase's mouth. I fix my gaze on my own glass and say, "Go on …"

He laughs but keeps staring at the glass in his hands.

"I came here because I wanted to get drunk and try to forget about you. I gave the bartender my phone to keep in his safe, so I wouldn't be able to call you once I'd started drinking." He finally looks over at me and puts his hand over his heart. "I love what you said just now."

"I'm pretty fond of what you're saying right now too."

I turn my body towards his, leaning forward, exposing my cleavage in a way that I don't normally do on purpose, but I don't typically want so badly to give my body to someone the way that I want to give myself to Chase McKay. Chase lowers his eyes, taking my curves in for just one wolfish second, but when he looks back up at me it's like a switch has been flipped.

"I can't say or do all the things I want to say and do to you in here, Aimee. Keaton still likes you, and I'm in here with him all the time. Let's get out of here. Let's say and do all the things we want to say and do to each other for one night. Tonight. Just tonight."

Those words, *tonight, just tonight,* echo around my brain and dance seductively all around me.

"What about Keaton?" I say it so quietly, because I don't really want to say it.

"He's in the Hamptons with someone until tomorrow morning."

"Oh. Well, good for him."

"This will be a one-night only event for us. We'll get it out of our systems. After tonight, we never speak of this again."

I clamp my lips together and then nod my head.

We stare at each other, and he can see in my eyes and the way my body relaxes, that my answer is *yes.* *Tonight, just tonight.* I don't know how I can possibly get enough of him in one night, but I will try.

Our hands slowly reach toward each other, and just when we're about to touch fingers, Roxy grabs my shoulders and shoves my jacket at me.

"Hey there, Chase McKay!" she exclaims as she pulls me away from him. "Off to the ladies' room—we'll be right back!"

I look back at Chase apologetically. He's rubbing his face with his hands, but he's smiling. If he's gone when we return from the ladies' room I will probably murder my roommate, but she'd probably understand.

As soon as the bathroom door is closed and Roxy has confirmed that no one is in the stall, she whisper-yells, "Okay, you need to take it down a notch, Miss Lady Wood. I could literally see your erect nipples from across the dimly-lit room. I keep expecting you to shoot laser beams from them."

"What? It's cold in here. You're the one who made me wear this! Wait—seriously?! *You're* telling me to take it down a notch? *You?*"

"I thought you had more control over your nips. You don't want him to think you don't have any respect for his best friend and business partner, right?"

"No. I mean, you're right." Every now and then, Roxy reminds me why she's a highly-paid executive.

"Yeah, well." She turns to the mirror and touches up her lip gloss. "You've got Wet Panty Face, my friend."

I cover my face. I'm not exactly sure what Wet Panty Face is, but I'm positive that I have it when I'm around Chase. "Shut up."

"So, I'm guessing you haven't told him about the j-o-b situation."

"I mean. Nothing's going to change between now and tomorrow. I'll tell him in the morning. Before we get to the office. Right?"

"Right! The only thing you need to tell that guy tonight is 'oh yeah, harder, more, right there, don't stop.'"

"I thought you wanted me to take it down a notch."

"I want you to slow things down up front, so he doesn't think you're being an idiot. And I want you to be a little more ladylike so he can remember that *he* was the one coming onto *you*. You know. Tomorrow, when you're at the office together."

"Okay wait, the fact that you're encouraging me to do this at all leads me to believe that it's a terrible idea."

"Whaaaaat? *Offense!* I am a renowned purveyor of common sense!"

"No. Shit. No. We can't do this."

Roxy grabs my wrist. "This was my bad. I shouldn't have pulled you away from him. You're fine. You deserve this."

"No. It's one thing to regret something you didn't do, but if we both regret what we *do* then we might not be able to bounce back from that—tomorrow at work—and what about Chase and Keaton and their relationship?"

"I believe the saying is: it's better to ask for forgiveness than to ask for permission."

"I don't need Keaton's permission!" I snap.

"Exactly. I mean, Chase might, but that's for him to deal with. *You* need to deal with your attraction to Chase. But don't listen to me, listen to your nipples. Listen to your panties. Listen to the way Chase looks at you. That boy is fire and your whole life you've been rubbing two wet sticks together with other guys, trying to create a spark." My friend is not just egging me on—for once, she is impassioned. She has tears in her eyes. "What is the point of moving to New York if you aren't going to take chances and live big in the moment and let every fucking day and night burn to the ground until all that's left is the beautiful memory of what you loved and what scared you?"

CHAPTER 5
CHASE

S he's mine.

I let her go and she came back to me.

All the feelings that I've tried to bury just demolished their shitty casket as soon as I saw Aimee's face again.

My dick has been trying to burst out of my jeans ever since I saw her in that deceptively sweet little blouse that's clinging to her even tighter than I want to cling to her.

I gave my friend his shot and he missed it. So fuck doing the right thing. I'm not going to overthink anything tonight. Tonight, I do what I want. And I want Aimee. I don't have a clue how I'll ever get enough of her in one night, but she will have all of me. One night in heaven will be easier to live with than the month I've spent in hell thinking I could never have her.

I'm about to enter uncharted territory with Keaton, but there's no one I'd rather be entering, more than

Aimee. I mean—entering into uncharted territory with. Never mind.

I doubt that I'll tell Keaton about it tomorrow, but I'll have to eventually, because I don't want to keep that kind of secret from him. But that's *after tonight*. First, we need to have our night to remember. All I want to do is take her to the nearest hotel and get her naked, but I need to make this last all night. I need to take her somewhere no one we know will see us together. I need to get her to a place where we can forget about yesterday and tomorrow and Keaton.

Denny finally comes over to check on me, eyebrow cocked, grin loaded. "Well now," he says. "Someone's night has taken a turn for the better."

"Time to settle-up," I say. No need for explanation.

"On the house as always," he insists.

"Thanks. I meant I can take my phone back now. I don't have to worry about saying the things that I want to say to her."

The fucker shakes his head. "No can do, friend. You said, 'no matter what.' I gave you my word." Yeah, this is why I came to Denny—I can trust him not to tell Keaton about any of this and I can trust him to keep his word to me even when I was being a giant pussy.

"I will give you another fifty bucks to forget about what I said earlier. Just get me my phone. Come on. I don't want to have to come back here in the morning."

"Can't do it. Sorry, man." He's not enjoying this. Being a man of honor means as much to him as it does to me. *Dick.*

I'm way too happy to put up a fight, so I'll just have

to leave Aimee a little earlier tomorrow to swing by and get it. "Fine," I say. "Am I gonna meet you here or at your place in the morning?"

"What time are we talking?"

"I don't know. Eight or nine?"

"I'll be at the gym."

"You better be."

When I see Roxy dragging Aimee out of the ladies' room, I know that something has shifted for her, but this train has already left the station. I will lean out as far as I have to and grab Aimee's hand to pull her back onboard. Roxy deposits her in front of me and then skips away.

I put my jacket on and I'm ready to go. "Let's get out of here."

"Really? Now? I mean. I probably shouldn't leave Roxy. She's a surprisingly fragile girl, she won't want me to leave without her, she's …"

"Leaving without you. Right now."

"What?" She snaps her head toward the door just as Roxy waves to us, her arm around the guy she's been sitting on since they arrived. Aimee looks down at her purse and pulls out her phone. "Oh. She's going home with him," she confirms. "She texted me his address."

"Good," I say. "That's smart."

"Yeah. She's a real wise lady."

"Let's get out of here."

"Like where?" She wrinkles her nose, smirking. "You want to take me to some motel in Queens, like I'm your dirty little secret?"

"Darlin', in half an hour you will *wish* I had taken you to a motel in Queens."

"That's strangely intriguing."

"You've got a jacket, yeah?

"Yeah. Roxy didn't want me to wear it, but I insisted. She dressed me tonight."

She looks down and re-fastens a little button that's come undone. I catch a guy ogling her and give him a look that makes him physically back off.

"I'm a big fan of Roxy's work, believe me, but you'll need that jacket." I take the jacket from her and hold it up so she can slip her arms into the sleeves. She looks back at me when I rest my hands on her shoulders for one second, two seconds, three.

I shove my hands into my jacket pockets to keep from throwing her over my shoulder and carrying her into the back office.

Make it last all night.

"How are those shoes you're wearing? Comfortable?"

"Comfortable enough."

"And you? You're comfortable? With this?"

She purses her lips again. Those full glossy lips that remind me of my youth and kisses that lasted days, those lips that look like they taste like strawberries, those lips that look like they could suck a dead man back to life. There's something she's not telling me, but after what she *has* told me, I don't know if anything else matters right now. She nods once. Affirmative. "Yes. Let's burn everything to the ground."

I like that. "Yes. Let's."

I want to take her hand and never let go, but not in here. I lead her to the door, hold it open and inhale the delicious scent of her as she passes through it. It's weird not having my phone on me, but this feels right. Walking out into this late spring night with this woman feels perfect.

The fact that I'm able to hail a cab right outside of Bitters just proves that we're doing the right thing at the right time. I hold the car door open for Aimee and she leans in so close to my face as she steps into the backseat, her grinning mouth inches from mine. *That dimple.* The whites of those eyes are glowing, and it makes the blue seem even darker somehow. I'm going to drown in those deep blue eyes tonight, but not until we both live a little first.

"To Coney Island, sir," I say to the driver. "Luna Park."

The driver grunts and nods and we're off.

I look over at Aimee, who's smiling and fastening her seatbelt.

"You ever been?"

"No, I haven't. I've been wanting to!"

"Well, you're gonna get what you want tonight."

I hold her hand now and I'm so aware of how my heart is racing when she whispers, "Yes. I hope you do too."

I'm dying to kiss her, but I'm not going to get too close until we're on the Parkway and no one can see us. It's not easy to hold back, but I've waited this long, I can wait a few more minutes. She weaves her fingers through mine and rests her head back.

"Have you been to Coney Island?"

"I haven't been since I was a teenager. We used to go pretty often when I was a kid. It's fun. In a weirdly beautiful, slightly dirty, all-American kind of way."

"Sounds appropriate." She bites her lower lip and she may as well have bitten mine. I feel it. I'm considering telling the driver to take us to the nearest hotel, when she asks: "What were you like when you were a teenager?"

"A lot like I am now, but skinnier and just a little bit reckless."

"Long hair?"

"Always. I promised my mom I'd never cut it short."

"Tattoos?"

"Tattoos are from the summer I spent in Ireland, between high school and Wharton."

She lowers her eyes for a second. She's thinking about how I met Keaton at Wharton, I know it. He probably told her about that. I tighten my grip on her hand.

"That was also the summer I picked up the smoking habit."

She looks up at me, smiling. "Did you really quit?"

"I really did."

"I'm really glad."

"Good. What were *you* like in high school?"

She sighs and fixes her apologetic eyes on mine. "A lot like I am now, but skinnier. And never as reckless as I wanted to be."

Fuck it—we're on a four-lane street. It's dark. No one will see us.

I take her sweet face in my hands and finally kiss that mouth. Soft and quick and then I pull back so I can watch as her eyelids close and her lips part. Her hand squeezes my thigh, and my hands are up in her thick, silky hair. She gently tugs on my lower lip with her teeth, an invitation and a dare, and I'm not aware of anything anymore. Nothing but the way she somehow manages to tease *and* satisfy me at the same time, with her lips and tongue and hands. Nothing but the way she makes me feel. Nothing but her.

I want her.

I want all of her.

I want to do everything with this woman, and we won't sleep until I have.

Her lips don't taste like strawberries, they taste like toffee and sherry and licorice and spice and lust and goodness and heaven and forever, and this is the best first taste of anything I've ever had.

CHAPTER 6
AIMEE

Only two things are holding me back from climbing on top of Chase McKay and dry humping him in the back of this cab—the seatbelt, and a vague memory of the job I was hired to start tomorrow. But that's it. My inherent need to be respected as a woman in the business world? Screw it! My sense of common decency? Gone! Lost it somewhere along Hamilton Avenue when those hands touched my face and I felt that soft full mouth on my mouth, and the hint of stubble around it tickling my skin.

He is the most sensual kisser I have ever had the pleasure of kissing, and I have never run my hands through such long hair while kissing someone before. I love it so much that for a split second I wonder if this means I'm a lesbian, and then I let one hand drop to his crotch and feel the magnificent rock-hard bulge in his jeans. Nope. I definitely like cock.

I definitely like Chase McKay.

He definitely likes that my hand is on that magnificent rock-hard bulge in his jeans, but he pulls away from me gently while smiling. "Hey, beautiful," he groans while adjusting himself, "we need to take it easy."

I cover my mouth in horror. There I go again, gulping it down when I should be savoring the first sip. "I'm so sorry!"

"Don't apologize. Believe me, I want to do this. Just not in the back of a cab on the way to Luna Park."

"Yes, no, totally," I say, smoothing down my hair and my blouse and generally trying to reassemble myself back into the kind of lady who doesn't molest hot guys in public. I can do that. Who's got two thumbs, complete control over her libido, and isn't going to put her hands on Chase McKay again until he begs her to?

This horny monkey.

I briefly make eye contact with the cab driver in the rearview mirror, but he seems pretty indifferent and I honestly don't think he'd care what we do back here as long we don't leave some sticky mess. Not that we'd ever—ever do that.

Probably.

I mean.

Maybe on the way *back* from Luna Park …

Chase laces his fingers with mine again, this time I can feel the tension in his arm as he tries to keep my hand where it is. Like I'm incapable of stopping myself from giving him a hand job or something. Lord, what he must think of me.

I am reminded of what Roxy said about making sure

he remembers that *he* was the one who made the first move tonight. Taking a very deep breath, I try to calm myself down. Only, I take such a deep breath that the top-fastened button of my ridiculously tight blouse actually flies off and hits the back of the driver's seat. Even my clothes are losing their shit around this man. I just stare down at the stupid little button on the dirty cab floor, hoping that maybe Chase didn't notice. He slowly reaches across my lap, down between my legs, to the floor, and then holds up the button between his thumb and index finger.

I try so hard not to laugh, but when I look over at Chase and see how amused he is, I just let loose. I take the button from him and toss it back onto the floor, because what's the point? This blouse, along with my dignity, will not survive the rest of the night. We both crack up. I've never heard him laugh like that before. His eyes are twinkling and there's pure joy dancing across his usually still face and torso.

Once the laughter has subsided, I say to him, "I really thought you hated me."

"I wish I could have." He squeezes my hand as he looks out the window. "I've never struggled with anything as much as this. Even quitting smoking cold turkey has been easier."

I let go of his hand and turn his face towards me. "I always wanted you, Chase," I whisper. "Always, always. I'm sorry. I know he's your best friend and your partner and I liked him, I really did, but it was always you that I wanted. If I could go back to that night and do it all over again ..."

He puts his hands over mine. "That's what we're doing now. It's not your fault at all. No more talking about Keaton tonight, okay?"

"Okay." I rest my forehead against his before pulling away. "It just kills me to know that you were suffering. I had no idea."

"No more talking about *before* tonight."

"Okay."

We remain silent, holding hands and looking out the window toward the water for the rest of the way. The sun is setting against cotton candy-colored clouds. I almost wish that there was more traffic, or that we were further from our destination, because this, even just this, feels good. But I am also quite certain that being there, or anywhere, with Chase will be great.

I haven't looked at the time since I checked my phone at the bar, because I don't want to be aware of time passing or the fact that at some point it won't be tonight anymore, and I'll have to deal with the Mother of all Mondays. But if everything that happens tonight matters so much, surely that means that what comes to light tomorrow won't matter *too* much? Right?

———

I can't believe I'm at an amusement park with Chase McKay. I feel like I'm in a Nicholas Sparks movie that's directed by Martin Scorcese, because this feels so time-less and romantic but also like I could get mugged or barfed on by a passing stranger at any moment. But if his goal was to help me feel young and reckless, then mission accomplished.

This noisy place is just bustling with youth and eager young love and sex. It's PDA Central. The air is so thick with teenage pheromones, I'm giddy. In the past twenty feet, from the entrance to where we're standing now, we've passed three young couples making out.

Chase and I are holding hands, and right now we're probably the most reserved people here. But then Chase stops and pulls me to him, his hand to the back of my neck, and he lays another one of those sensual kisses on me. I nearly lose my balance, but he's got me. He's got such a hold on me that everything around us is just bright spinning lights. I don't know if it's the neon lights of Luna Park or the sparks flying from my brain. I hear some guys hoot and holler. They could be hooting and hollering at us, or any number of other young kissing couples, but we are definitely one of the young kissing couples now.

I am still clinging to his leather jacket when Chase slowly pulls his lips from mine and says: "Come on. Let's do the Cyclone first. You like rollercoasters?"

"Of course! You want to start with the main attraction, huh?"

He kisses me again, quick and hard. "Tonight I do." He leads me in the direction of The Cyclone, running. I laugh while trying to keep up with him. He could have said, "Come on, let's go get our legs sawed off!" and I would still follow.

The old wooden rollercoaster is a historic Coney Island landmark. I stop to take a picture of it with my phone, text it to Roxy so she knows where I am, although I'm sure the guy from the bar is balls-deep inside of her by now. I thank Chase for paying for the ride, and we snake around to the end of the surprisingly short line. I shudder when I hear the *clack clack clack* of the rising cars and the loud rattling of the rails when they head down. Chase watches me and squeezes my hand.

"You nervous?"

"Not really, but I've never been on a wooden roller-coaster before. It looks like I might need to make a chiropractor appointment after, but I'd imagine it's like two minutes of awesome rough sex." I manage to refrain from covering my mouth after mentioning sex, because it's just so obvious that it's taking over my mind.

"If you need a chiropractor after rough sex, then you haven't been doing it with the right guys." He declares this as he looks up at the structure, a throwaway line.

Meanwhile, I'm swallowing my tongue.

He's definitely right about that, but I'm not going to say anything. I have not been doing it with the right guys. In Ann Arbor, it was college boys and men who were great at navigating the stock market and speaking foreign languages but who could not find my clitoris or G-spot or recognize a fake orgasm.

I'm shuddering again, for different reasons.

The anticipation is killing me.

When it's our turn to board, we're ushered to the front seat and Chase seems pleased with this arrangement. He winks at me as the safety bar is lowered. I grip the bar in front of me, but Chase says, "It's better if you don't hold onto the bar. Your muscles can get all wrenched up. You gotta let go and trust the ride."

And I do.

The ascent, combined with the panoramic view of the park and the beach and the *clack clack clack* and the unnerving lurch forward, have my pulse racing, but it's the adrenaline rush of the steep fall and the ensuing stomach drop that I will always associate with this night and Chase McKay. I let out a high-pitched scream and for the first time ever, my hands are up in the air as I surrender to the g-force and the universe and the engineers who designed this thing.

I can handle anything!

Hot sex with a hot guy that I barely know!

Delicate personal and business situations!

More hot sex with a hot guy that I barely know!

By the time we're done being jostled and jolted, I am so damned excited and aroused that when I get off that roller coaster, I don't even bother trying to get my bearings on solid ground. I throw my arms around Chase's neck and kiss him with wild abandon, until the attendant clears his throat and asks us to move along.

My date for the evening is quietly laughing and shaking his head as we exit through the turnstile gate, but as soon as we're through, he grabs my hand and we're running down the dimly-lit road towards the boardwalk. I am drunk on so much more than three beers and a shot of Irish whiskey. I'm drunk on Chase McKay and not even remotely worried about the hangover that's coming tomorrow.

CHAPTER 7
CHASE

'm a big fan of bringing a woman to the brink, but I also know when a woman needs to come, and Aimee Gilpin is on the verge of mounting me in front of a crowd of tourists if I don't do something to satisfy her immediately.

The boardwalk is well-lit and there's a fair amount of people strolling around—not as many as in the summer. But the beach is nearly deserted, and I know a dark corner where we (probably) won't get knifed by a junkie. I pull her around the corner of a small public building at the edge of the beach, to a covered area with some privacy from most angles. The building is locked at night, and let's just say that I got lucky here once when I was skinny teenager who was more reckless than I am now. Now that I've been to law school, I'm scrolling through potential misdemeanors in my brain, before all the blood up there heads south.

Aimee is breathless when we reach our destination and I push her up against the brick wall.

"You ready to come for me, Aimee?"

She answers with loud gasps and moans into my mouth, wet frantic kisses, her hands grabbing at my hair like she's drowning. I hike her up and her legs wrap effortlessly around my waist. Hard as steel and pressing against her, I let out a growl as I grind upwards, tugging at that long hair and letting her suck on my tongue.

I don't know if this is what she's like with all men or if she just hasn't gotten any in a while, and I don't care. She's hot and it's going to hurt like a mother to keep myself from coming in my jeans like a twelve-year-old. I've basically been a walking six-foot-two erection.

"I'm not usually like this I swear," she whispers into my ear before biting and sucking on my earlobe.

"I am not judging you right now, believe me."

"No but I need you to know that."

"Shhh. You have to stay quiet."

She nods, but she's shaking all over and I know she isn't cold. A little high-pitched animal sound comes out of her mouth and I nearly laugh.

Maneuvering her so her feet are on the ground again, I undo the button and zipper of her jeans, pull them down a bit and cover her mouth with one hand while the other finds its way into her panties. I'm glad I'm covering her mouth, because she lets loose a little squeal that's not quite as loud as the ones she made when we were on the Cyclone, but I have to fight to keep my groans low when I feel just how warm and wet she is for me. Her hips are rolling and crashing against me like the waves less than half a mile from us, her hands keep grasping at my jacket as I rub and flutter against her clit until finally she just rests her hands on top of her head. I fully expect the rest of the buttons to pop off of her blouse, because her tits are straining to break free, and feeling them against my chest is driving me insane. When my two fingers slide inside of her, she clenches around them immediately, her head falls back and then she's kissing the palm of my hand while I muffle the sound of her passionate yeses and wails.

"Shhhhh."

This is so the opposite of how I saw things going when I got up this morning and I have never been so happy about being wrong.

Everything about this woman and this moment feels right.

I thrust my fingers in and out fast while my thumb works her clit. I need to make her come quickly, and that's all it takes to make her tense up and then start vibrating harder than she did on the roller coaster. I keep my hand still in place until her aftershocks die down, while trying to calm my own breaths. I can't wait to hear these noises she's making later, when she doesn't have to hold back.

I remove my hand from Aimee's mouth and press my mouth against hers.

Her breathing is long and loud and deep, and it's too dark to see if she's flushed or not, but how could she not be.

I slowly pull my fingers out. She sighs and her hands drop to her sides. She licks her lips and rolls her head around before zipping up her jeans.

"Well, I'm having a really fun night so far," she whispers.

We both crack up and I have to go for a quick little pace back and forth before we return to the oblivious crowds.

———

Aimee has barely said a word since we walked from the boardwalk to the Nathan's Famous cart by the Wonder Wheel. She has definitely worked up an appetite. She's chowing down on her hot dog and sucking on her lemonade straw so hard that I might have to go for another walk to get rid of the bulge that's trying to break out of my pants. I can tell she's embarrassed, and I don't want her to feel anything but good.

A change of subject might do the trick.

"You ever heard the story of Deno and the Wonder Wheel?"

She shakes her head and I nearly forget the story I'm about to tell her when I watch her lick the mustard from the side of her lips.

I clear my throat and continue. "Deno Vourderis was born in Greece, 1920. Family emigrated here when he was a teenager and his first job was selling hot dogs from his dad's pushcart in Manhattan. He meets Lula, also here from Greece, and they spend their dates around Coney Island in the summer. One day, in the 1940s, he proposes to her and says, 'I don't have money for a ring right now, but if you turn and look at that big wheel over there, I promise that one day I'll buy that for you. A ring so big that everyone in the world can see how much I love you.'"

Aimee's deep blue eyes are tearing up. I haven't cried since I was five, but it moves me. Something about this woman moves me, more than music, more than my drive to succeed, more than loyalty. That something is lovely and delicate but dangerous—a poisonous flower that could bring me to my knees.

The deep blues look to me to continue, so I do. "Deno eventually gets a job fixing the kiddie rides here, and in 1983 he buys the Wonder Wheel for two hundred fifty-thousand dollars. They restored it. Deno and Lula had four kids, and his family still runs the Wonder Wheel and the amusement park around it. Sweet, huh?"

She exhales. "That is so sweet. I love that story."

"There are a lot of stories like that, about immigrants living the American dream around here. That's probably the most famous one in Coney Island. That's why I love small businesses."

She nods. "Me too."

I wait for her to ask me about my business, but she doesn't, which is fine. Pretty hard to talk about it without talking about Keaton. While she's finishing up her lemonade, I ask, "Hey, I heard you got laid-off a few weeks ago. You doing okay?"

Her eyes widen and she starts choking. She covers her mouth. I rub her back.

"You alright?"

She nods while coughing a few times, her eyes are tearing up again.

"I'm fine," she says, her voice tight and hoarse.

Finally, she's able to answer. "I got a bit of severance, and I had a really good interview the other day, so I'm … hopeful that it will all work out."

"That's great. Well, I hope it works out, but let me know if you need help. I can ask around. What is it you specialize in, exactly? You're a business consultant, right?"

She looks around, almost as if she's looking for a distraction. "Yeah, where do we throw these away?" She takes my trash from me and deposits everything in the nearest bins. "Oh hey!" she exclaims, when she spots the Zoltar Speaks machine. "This is that thing from the movie *Big*!" She's so excited, it's pretty cute.

"Yeah, but it's not exactly like the one in the movie," I say, walking over to join her. "You don't make a wish, but you do pay him a buck for a fortune. Wanna try?"

"Well, let me get this," she says, reaching inside her purse and feeding a dollar into the machine before I can protest.

The creepy animatronic fortune teller comes to life, his hand moving around the crystal-looking ball in front of him inside the glass box. "Zoltar is here, to give you the wisdom of the ancients," he says in some exotic accent. "Do with it what you will!" He then advises us to live each day as if it's our last, because one day it will be, and suggests giving him more money for more instructions, then the machine spits out a card. She gestures for me to take it.

"All yours," I tell her.

She pulls it out of the slot and reads it, smiling and biting her lower lip.

"What's it say?"

She holds the card to her chest and grins at me. "It's a secret." She puts it into her purse. "We going on the Wonder Wheel?"

"Hell, yeah."

———

"You ready to rock?" I ask her, while we settle into the big metal cage. It's not too busy, so we're able to have the whole swinging car to ourselves. As we take the back seat, I put my arm around her shoulder and she leans into me. This feels right. This feels perfect.

"This isn't like a normal Ferris wheel, is it?" she asks.

"Kinda." I shrug.

She punches my shoulder. "That's not an answer."

For the first few seconds, we're lifted up, and she coos at the pretty view of the park. Then all of a sudden the car slides forward really fast and then back again. It's very unnerving. She squeals and swears and it's awesome. It keeps swinging in place for a while, and she puts her hand on my thigh and smiles at me.

When the car slides forward again she laughs gleefully.

On our second round, while hanging out near the top, a young woman in the car in front of us squeals. Aimee squeezes my leg and tries to see if the woman is okay, but it's too dark. Then we hear her scream: "I'm engaged!   We're   fucking   engaged,   people! Wooohooooo!"

Aimee yells out: "Congratulations!"

"Thank you!" the woman yells back. "He just asked me to marry him up here!"

"That's so romantic!" Aimee yells. "That's so cute," she says to me. She seems to be genuinely happy for these total strangers that we can't even see.

When we get off the ride, this young couple is hugging, and the girl is telling the guy to take a selfie of them with her camera so she can hold her ring finger up.

Aimee goes over and asks if they want her to take pictures for them.

"Yaaaasssss!" the girl says.

Aimee takes the phone from her and touches her hand and gushes over the ring. I stand out of the way and just watch as my date talks to these people and takes a hundred pictures of them like she's known them forever. This woman? She's beautiful inside and out.

Years from now, I'm sure I'll remember this as the moment when I really fell in love with her.

But right now, all I can think about is how I need to get this woman to a hotel so I can see how beautiful she is underneath those clothes and worship every inch of her.

CHAPTER 8
AIMEE

Chase is really serious about not wanting to take any chances on running into Keaton, even though he's supposed to be in the Hamptons. That rules out either of our apartments, so he has checked us into a pretty big hotel by the Brooklyn Bridge, that both of us could walk home from in the morning. He is just as thoughtful about people's time and feelings as he is about making me come when I desperately need that release.

We are also not far from the downtown Brooklyn offices of SnapLegal-NYC, where we will both have a meeting tomorrow.

But I'm not going to think about that now.

That's *after tonight*.

A Sunday night in mid-June, the lobby is fairly quiet but not empty. As we wait for the elevator doors to open and take us to the executive room with a king bed, he snakes his arm around my waist and draws me closer to him. Ever since the Wonder Wheel, he hasn't said much, but his constant touch has grown more urgent and possessive and I love it. His fingers find an area of exposed skin beneath my short jacket, where my ridiculous blouse and camisole are pulling away from the top of my jeans. Just the pads of his fingers on my waist send little shockwaves through me.

When the elevator dings, it's speaking for me. *Ding! I'm done. Thoroughly-heated. Ready to be consumed.*

He leads me inside, presses a button and waits for the doors to slide shut before gently pushing my back up against the mirrored wall. His face is so close to mine, one hand resting lightly on my hip, the other tracing my jaw, his thumb brushing across my lower lip. Then his index finger lightly traces the scalloped edge of my camisole, barely touching the skin of my heaving bosom. All of my nerve endings are on high alert. All of me wants him.

I have never craved another person like this before. Every single one of the trillions of cells in my body are begging—not for food, air and water—but for him.

The tiny space between us, the gentle tentativeness, the way he's staring into my eyes is driving me wild, but I am determined to take it slow. I am determined to prove to both of us that I am a sensual woman. I am not merely the horny-as-fuck-orgasm-deprived girl who rode his hand behind some building on the beach about an hour ago.

His mouth hovers a few millimeters above mine when we reach our floor. I grin and push him aside, grab his hand and let him lead me to the door. Taking me to Coney Island and then bringing me to a hotel was a brilliant idea, because everyone knows that hotel sex is the best sex there is. Everyone knows this. Even people like me, who've never had hotel sex before.

When I emerge from the bathroom, I'm wearing only my blouse, camisole and panties. We sensual women try to save time by removing our shoes and skinny jeans ourselves, when time with a hot guy is limited. I find Chase waiting for me, in the dimly-lit room. He has turned on music, and he's resting his butt against the desk. He has removed his jacket. While I do love that sexy black leather motorcycle jacket, seeing his inked arms does unexpected things to me.

There's so much I want to know about this man, but it seems like all I need to know now is that we are here for each other's pleasure, and I will give and get as much as I can in the next few hours.

Chase's hands grip the edge of the desk as he scans the lower half of my body. I love the way he looks at me, as if I'm the only thing he sees. He studies me, but not like some men do, where you can tell they're just trying to figure out how to manipulate you. Chase reads me the way you read a book that you can't put down, and I feel myself becoming a more interesting book because of it.

When I stop to stand about a foot in front of him, I reach for the bottom of his white T-shirt, and he lets me pull it up over his head. I run my hands along the tattoos on each of his arms, the design across the top of his smooth olive-toned chest, and caress his taut pecs and abs. It looks like he's been spending extra time at the gym, probably to keep from smoking. A win, for both of us.

"You're beautiful," I tell him. I've never said that to a man before, never thought that about a man that I've met.

He says nothing, but he's smiling with his eyes, his beautiful brown eyes.

I touch my fingertips to his full mouth, that beautiful mouth made just for kissing.

His hands meet at the small of my back and bring me in a little bit closer.

I lay a tender kiss on his cheek, his neck, his collarbone.

My lips softly graze his, as I unbutton and unzip his jeans.

He makes a deep, guttural sound when my hand reaches inside his boxer briefs. He is so hard for me, but he's patiently letting me explore him like this and it's such a turn-on. I nibble on his lower lip while slowly stroking the hot length of him. A light easy grasp at first, and then I grip him harder. He squeezes my ass and massages my hips, taking his time, but I can literally feel the restless passion growing. When the palm of my hand twists over the head of his cock, he growls. His eyes are so hooded, I can barely see his irises.

"How you feeling about this little blouse of yours?"

"I'm feeling like it's about time you tore it apart."

The remaining buttons pop off when Chase rips the fabric and liberates me from it.

He takes hold of my breasts, squeezes, gently bites

my flesh before pulling the camisole off and tossing it aside. I lean back, letting him hold me up, offering myself to him. His warm tongue does heavenly, devastating things to my nipples. They have been stiff and straining for him all night, and now that they have him, the rest of my body is shocked by how satisfying this is. He is ravenous, and I would give him anything, but I'm also so aware that he is always giving to me.

My whole adult life, my body has been some kind of carnal vending machine for the men I've been with, but this man, *this man* … I am being feasted upon while he simultaneously lavishes me with treats.

I am about to tell him not to stop, never stop, when he maneuvers me so that I am now the one who's leaning back against the desk, gripping the edge of it.

He's whispering things, as his lips travel downwards.

The words don't quite register in my brain, but I understand him anyway.

You're so beautiful.

You are so fucking sexy.

This is mine, and this is mine, and this is mine.

He pulls down my panties, letting me step out of them, and moves my leg to rest on his shoulder as he kneels in front of me while muttering something about getting comfortable and holding on tight because he's going to be down here for a while.

The first time he licks my entrance, it is so delicate it tickles.

The second time he does it, he is more voracious, and I clench up, drawing in a breath.

The third time he does it, he is savoring me, and I shudder, surrendering to the warmth of his mouth and tongue.

Oh God, he's circling, making a figure-eight around my clit with his tongue while his finger slowly strokes up and down the sides of my inner lips. My head rolls, back arches, my hands reach for his hair. My pelvis starts rocking, everything down there is so engorged, the tension is unbearable.

As if reading my clitoris's mind, Chase applies pressure by sucking on it. The sudden shock of it is electrifying in its pleasure-pain and unlike anything I've ever felt before. I scream out. The sound of him enjoying what he's doing down there just adds to the agonizing ecstasy. He grabs onto my ass to hold me down, because I feel like I could take flight, but he is grounding himself and going deeper with his tongue, penetrating and thrusting and flicking.

There is nothing left in this world besides my vulva and this man's mouth.

This, only this.

Oh God, oh God, Chase!

I've lost control. Both of my thighs are squeezing tight around his neck, and I really hope I'm not strangling him, but he seems to be invigorated. I've never been tongue-fucked before—I didn't know that was a thing!

Oh my lord, is it ever a thing.

There is nothing better than this.

I'm slammed with full-body convulsions.

The noises that are coming from my throat are loud and deep, and then they are operatic.

When I feel his fingernails dig into the flesh of my ass, I get a jolt, and he responds by gently swirling his tongue around and then keeping his hand there while I let the waves of rapture wash over me. He slows things down while keeping it going. I'm still feeling after-shocks, stuck in a state of bliss.

He licks and bites and sucks on my inner thigh and then somehow manages to carry me to the bed while my legs are wrapped around his neck, supporting my back while my head and arms dangle lifelessly from my torso. Like this is some erotic dance performance, and maybe it is.

I am sprawled out, eyes closed, elated and so very sated.

His voice is gruff when he says, "You ready for more, beautiful?"

I somehow manage to open my eyes and see that he is hovering over me, massive erection sheathed in a condom, a heat-seeking missile aimed straight at me.

"Oh God, yes!" I bend my legs on either side of him.

He teases the opening before slowly, so slowly, pressing inside of me. Being filled up with him is a burning delight, his cock a monument that I expand myself for, in order to completely experience and worship it. He goes deep and gets comfortable in there, before pulling out and going deeper, still hovering over me, waiting to make sure that I can handle him. All of him. I give him the go ahead by raising my hips. His groan is a shotgun fired, and we are off to the races.

His thrusts are punishing but graceful, I cry out with each thump of the headboard, moving in rhythm with him.

His hair hangs down around my face like curtains, his own face mostly in shadows, but the sound of him exerting himself and moaning is all I need.

He starts pumping harder and faster, and just when I think he must be reaching a climax, he pulls out, flips me over, draws me up onto my knees and enters me from behind. He squeezes my breasts while I clutch onto the bedspread and let this animal side of him take over while I enjoy the entirely new sensation of being penetrated from this angle.

Holy crap, that must be my G-spot!

The dull burgeoning pleasure is like nothing I've ever felt before.

This … *this* … there is nothing better than this.

I lean down on my forearms, and that small adjustment makes Chase squeeze me harder, plow into me faster.

When he slaps my ass, it sends a surge of excitement through me.

I don't know who I am anymore, except a woman who has just discovered that she likes to be spanked during sex.

"You like that?"

"Yeah, I like it."

He does it again.

I slowly realize that I'm having the kind of soul tingling, life-altering full-body orgasm that I thought was just a myth.

He grabs onto my hips and pulls me down toward the foot of the bed. My stomach is flat on the mattress and he holds me up by my hips while plunging down into me, hard and fast and then hard and slow. The groan that he makes while he tenses up and empties himself is the sexiest thing I've ever heard. He remains still and standing, holding me up like that for a few seconds, and then collapses onto my back, both of our legs bent and hanging off the edge of the bed. He pushes my hair to one side, to plant kisses along my shoulders. Our breaths are in sync. His hands cover mine.

I'm not sure how much time passes before he kisses the back of my head and tells me he'll be right back.

Crawling further up onto the bed, I turn over onto my back and close my eyes for a moment, blissed-out and smiling.

I must have drifted off to sleep for a few minutes, but I can sense that he's there when I wake up.

I'm all sultry and languid, lying here on the bed like a nude model in a Klimt painting. I feel like I'm composed of spinning circles and wavy lines, surrounded by a gold halo and vibrantly-colored flow-ers, a tree of life.

I can't even lift my head up to look at him, but my hand searches for him.

I need to touch him.

You did this to me.

What have you done?

I want more.

My hunger for him is insatiable. It's surprising and

overwhelming and terrifyingly unfamiliar. Maybe it's a good thing if we only have tonight. I don't know that my body could even handle much more of this.

But then again—before tonight, was this body of mine ever truly alive?

I know the answer to that, and the real question is: how can it possibly go on living without him?

CHAPTER 9
CHASE

"No one has ever made me feel this good," she says, her voice like honey. "Ever, ever." I rest my head on her belly and she tugs at my hair, giving me a little scalp massage.

"You're an incredibly stunning and sexy woman, you know that?"

I hear air blow out her nostrils. She finds that amusing, but I couldn't be more serious. The way she responds to me—it's like my body knew as soon as I saw her that it would be like this. Maybe my brain knew it too and was afraid of it. I don't feel vulnerable, exactly, but it has been a long time since I've felt this way. If I'm being honest, it's never been quite like this.

"More Than This" comes on the hotel satellite radio. I dig this song, but I've never felt it more than I do right now. I stroke her calf with one hand, exhausted and so satisfied and almost ready for more. I don't want to sleep. I have a meeting in the morning, so I need to sleep, but I'm not going to waste one second of this night with Aimee.

I hear her sniffle.

"You want me to turn off the air conditioning?"

"No, I'm fine," she says, her voice all gravelly now. She wipes her eyes.

I sit up to look at her.

"Are you crying?"

"No. Yes. It's so dumb."

"What's wrong?"

"Nothing. Nothing at all. This night has just been so … much. I'm happy, that's all."

"Good."

She pats my arm, reassuringly. It's a sweet gesture, but it made her tits jiggle a bit, and now I can't take my eyes off of them. I drag my fingertips down the center of her torso, collar bone to pelvis. She shivers. "Tell me something about you. Anything. Do your parents live here?"

"Yeah. They have an Italian restaurant in Park Slope. Had it my whole life. My mom's the chef, my dad's the manager. So if you ever want a Guinness with your organic rigatoni, go to Graziella."

She laughs. "Graziella. I like that. Did you ever work there?"

"All the time, until I was in high school and got too busy with other stuff."

"Busy being a little reckless?"

"A little of that, but mostly busy doing homework and making money for college. My parents could no longer afford me at that point."

She sits up carefully, so that my head drops from her belly to her lap, and those perfect tits are now hanging directly above my face.

"Okay, I have another question. I hope this isn't rude, but I'm so curious."

I think I say "Go on," but all I'm thinking is *get in my mouth.*

"How could you afford Wharton *and* law school? That's so much tuition."

A beautiful naked woman who wants to discuss my money-making skills? Where am I, and can I stay here forever?

"Combination of savings, stock investments, scholarships, fellowships. I worked really hard."

"That's impressive." She eyes my cock, which is a fucking flag pole right now, practically waving at her. "That is also very impressive."

In one second flat I've got her pinned down underneath me. She squeals, but soon realizes that it's going to be slow and steady this time around. I kiss her jaw, her neck, her shoulder, her collar bone, the notch between collar bones. I plant kisses all the way down the center of her and back up to her breasts, licking delicately until she's shuddering and wriggling around and whimpering. I let the strands of my hair tickle her skin while I explore every single inch of her with my mouth and my hands, top to bottom, front and back.

This is mine, and this is mine, and this is mine.

Tonight, tonight, tonight.

Mine.

When I'm kissing the arch of her right foot, she mutters, "Get inside me now, fuck, please!"

Well, since she said 'fuck.'

She grabs hold of my face when I'm gliding inside of her. It's so slick in there, but that gasping sound she makes as I fill her up, while she's kissing me, turns me on even more. I swear, I'm a bigger man for her than I've ever been.

Her arms and legs are wrapped around me so tightly. I'm so deep in her but it seems like I can't ever get deep enough for either of us. I feel this strange primal need to become a part of her. Not just to make my mark on her, but to live inside this woman, some-how. Create a third person that's not her or me, but some being that we become when we're together. This is entirely new but also feels like coming home.

"Chase, Chase, Chase!"

God, the way she says my name like I'm her savior or her master.

I'm the one who's surrendering myself to her.

Drowning and being reborn in the depths of her.

Union.

That's what this is.

This is what it's meant to be.

I can feel her orgasm slowly take over her, a tidal wave.

That movement ignites something and the wild beast in me takes hold of my body, soul and mind.

I lied.

I do want to make my mark on her.

She's mine.

Not just for tonight.

The explosion of energy from my center rips me apart and destroys everything that isn't us in this moment.

I'm unhinged.

I've lost control.

Everything goes black, and I am magnificent fucking nothingness, for less than a minute or for infinity, I don't know anything anymore.

When I come to, I'm lying still on top of her, two sweaty bodies breathing in tandem, returning to the room.

She says nothing, I say nothing.

I'm twenty-seven years old and this is the first time I've had sex with a woman that I love since I was seventeen.

Whoa.

What am I saying?

I barely know her.

It's too soon to really call this love. Isn't it?

I don't know what to call it yet, but I do know this: There are two lines that divide my adult life—the one that divides the time before and after I formed my company, and the one that divides the time before and after I spent the night with Aimee Gilpin. I have no idea what *after tonight* will look or feel like, but I know what's changed. I know I've changed. I may have been able to give up an insidious ten-year habit out of sheer force of will, but there is no way I can live the rest of my life without this woman.

AFTER TONIGHT

CHAPTER 10
CHASE

t's a great fucking morning.

My body feels raw and wrecked and alive and I am so fucking optimistic, I don't even care that I don't have time to pick up my phone from Denny. I'll catch up with him at some point today. It's more important for me to get to the office and have a face-to-face talk with Keaton. This can't wait. No more treating that fucker with kid gloves when it comes to Aimee. When it comes to Aimee—she's mine. That's all there is to it. He needs to know it, so I can let her and the world know it too.

Neither of us wanted to sleep last night, but the human body will only gift you with a certain number of orgasms before demanding sleep as payment for services rendered. Even after shower sex. I bolted awake at nearly eight o'clock. No sun was streaming through the windows because of the blackout curtains, and only the faintest traffic sounds could be heard outside. In the dim light of the bedside lamp, I watched

Aimee sleeping and didn't want to wake her. She didn't mention having a job or an interview today, so I figured I should let her sleep in.

I left her a note on the hotel stationary, telling her to order whatever she wants from room service and to take her time getting up because I told the front desk not to send up housecleaning until noon. In the note, I told her that last night was the best night of my life, and that I would call her once I got my phone back. I wrote that I want to see her again tonight, and the next night, and the next. I told her that I plan to tell Keaton about us as soon as possible.

I kissed the crown of her head and then left. Her hair was still a little bit damp from the shower, all spread out across the pillow. Wavy. Her hair must be naturally wavy. If I had my phone on me, I'd have taken a picture for her. She looks more wild and reckless like that.

She certainly seemed reckless to me.

I had been dreading the "after tonight" part, but the bandage will be ripped off.

Life will go on, and it will be fucking amazing.

Keaton and I are best friends because he likes that I give it to him straight. "Straight no Chaser," he always says. I'm going to give it to him straight today, whether he likes it or not.

Me, I like that Keaton's a bold-as-balls risk-taker, even though he needs to be reined-in half the time. He balances out my own heart and brain-motivated choices. I overthink. He overspends, overacts, overreacts.

We're a good team, and putting up with his entitled rich kid idiosyncrasies is a small price to pay, most of the time. He's had my back and I've had his, ever since we met at Wharton. While I was at law school, Keaton was partying and investing in real estate and the stock market with his trust fund money. He tried to convince me to drop out and launch my startup before anyone else did something similar, but I stood my ground. Having a lawyer CEO would give clients more confidence in the company, and I knew my patience would pay off. I never planned to take the bar exam or become a practicing lawyer, but having that NYU law degree is worth its weight in gold. By the time I'd gotten it, Keaton had made a couple of bad investments and he needed a win. He had always wanted to fund my startup because he knew it was a great idea and he helped me select a good group of co-investors. I agreed to back him as my Chief Financial Officer. It's not that I felt that I owed him for letting me live with him in Philadelphia—I just think he's a good partner for me when it comes to business, and I know how good he is at dealing with all of the investor bullshit that doesn't interest me.

SnapLegal-NYC is legal tech for small businesses. We provide affordable on-demand à la carte legal advice, plus low-cost legal services for local businesses. It's not robo-lawyers, it's real people and low overhead. The lawyers work remotely but they can use our offices whenever they need to. It may not be a big sexy startup idea, but I saw the need for it at my parents' restaurant and all the other storefronts in the neighborhood, and we've had steady growth ever since we launched.

Keaton wanted to go global, I insisted on staying local until we'd built up more of a reputation. He wanted to lease a huge premium converted loft space in Williamsburg, I got him to compromise on a fairly large kickass space in downtown Brooklyn, which my buddy Vince's brokerage helped us find. The one thing we've both agreed on in the last year is that it's time to switch to a subscription-based business model. It's never an easy transition, but it will lead to more revenue, sooner rather than later. We've hired a consultant to help us with the transition, and it all starts today.

By the time I get to our offices after changing clothes at home, it's after nine-thirty. We have a meeting with Elaine Hoffman and the project manager she's assigned to us at ten. I've never gotten to the office after nine unless I had a breakfast meeting first. I see Keaton's assistant, Nora, peeking in to see if I'm at my desk.

Why does the CFO have an assistant while my CTO and I don't, one might ask? Because my CTO and I agreed it was better for our budget to hold off on assistants for the first couple of years, but Keaton is paying Nora out of his own pocket because he would disappear up his own asshole if he didn't have a babysitter/wrangler around and I'm not going to do that job full-time.

When Nora sees me, she gives me a look that speaks

volumes. Keaton's already here and why the fuck am I not answering my cell phone? Nora is barely over five feet tall, but she could knock you on your ass with one of her looks. The girl knows who signs her checks, and I've learned to stay on her good side—which is why I stopped by her favorite coffee shop and brought her a latte and a scone.

"Forget to charge your phone, Chase *McCan'tanswer-hisfuckingphone?*" she says this while reaching for the coffee and taking a bite of the scone.

"That was weak, but good morning to you too, sunshine. He in his office?"

"Yes, please get him out of there, he's driving me crazy."

I had been planning to check messages first, but I might as well let that wait, at this point. I didn't see any frantic emails earlier, so there can't be anything more urgent than what I have to say to Keaton.

"Hey," Nora says, her mouth full. "Don't not be here when you're usually here. It pisses me off and everything goes to shit."

I look around to confirm that nothing at all appears to have gone to shit.

"Right. Your grammar is shit. Get to work."

"I have been working. *You* get to work."

I stare her down until she withers.

"Thank you for the coffee and scone, Mr. McKay."

"Atta girl."

I drop off my laptop in my office and cross the open space to Keaton's, saying 'hi' to the five engineers who are situated at a long bank of desks between us.

I find Keaton pacing back and forth in front of his desk, while scrolling through his phone. "Dude. What the fuck?"

"I don't have my phone on me—I'll get it back after work."

"Christ, I thought Greg and I would have to do this meeting without you."

"It's just a quick introductory meeting, you can relax. We hired them to do the hard stuff, remember?"

He cracks his neck. "I don't know why I'm so anxious today."

Because you obviously didn't have as much hot sex as I did this weekend.

"You wanna grab a quick coffee downstairs?"

"Yeah, let's do that."

I figure my best play is to take him to the café downstairs, give him the news about me and Aimee in a public place where he won't lose his shit, and then hustle up to our meeting so he has a chance to cool down before we discuss it any further. It's not that I'm scared of the guy, it's that I care more about this company than he does. I need his support at board meetings, but I also can't have him quitting or stirring up any kind of trouble before we go into our next round of funding.

I slap him on the back as we head out of his office.

"I can't believe you don't have your phone. You never lose your phone."

"Yeah, well. I had an unbelievable weekend. How about you?"

"It was okay. What'd you get up to?"

"Tell you in a minute."

I signal to my Chief Technology Officer, Greg Lee, that we'll be right back. When I'm looking into his office, I hear Keaton say, "Holy shit," under his breath as he stops in his tracks. When I look up to see what he sees, I say and do the exact same things.

Aimee Gilpin is standing around the waiting area by the entrance to our offices, looking around. From the neck down, she's all put-together in a pencil skirt and tucked-in blouse, but her hair looks like she's just driven around town in a convertible at high-speed and she appears to be even more anxious than Keaton was just now. I have no idea what she's doing here, but she doesn't look like she had even half as good a time as I did last night and that's troubling.

My first instinct is to grab her and take her up to the roof deck so I can do my best to get her relaxed. Fortunately, I remember who's beside me. Unfortunately, I'm standing next to an idiot.

"She wants me. I knew it," he whispers out of the side of his mouth, as he pulls down the cuffs on his Tom Ford dress shirt.

I almost want to laugh, but mostly I want to punch him in the head.

When Aimee sees us together, those lips that I've come to know and love subtly form the words, "oh shit."

Keaton strides toward her. Hearing him say her name makes me want to punch him in the kidneys, but I hang back so he can't see me shake my head at Aimee and mouth: "I haven't told him yet."

She barely nods, signaling that she understands, and manages to gracefully hold her hand out to shake Keaton's while he's clearly moving in for a cheek kiss.

"Aren't you a sight for sore eyes on a Monday morning," my Chief Fuckhead Officer says.

"Hey there—*both of you!* Good to see you, great … good … great."

I think I can see all of her teeth. She sort of looks like she's losing her mind.

"You remember my buddy, Chase?" Keaton pats me on the shoulder and I want to punch him in the throat.

"How's it going?" I say, as I shake her moist hand. That hand did amazing things to me for hours. As soon as she yanks it away from me, I know that I probably should have woken her up to say goodbye before I left the hotel. That's on me.

"Let me guess," Keaton says, as he puts his fucking arm around her shoulder. "You've had time to reconsider and you've decided you want to go with me to *Wicked*. You're in luck—"

She interrupts him, thank God, while stepping away from him. "Actually, I thought it would be a good idea for me to show up before Elaine Hoffman gets here, so I can tell you guys that *I* am going to be the project manager overseeing your transition to subscription services. It's my specialty, and I have a great track record. She hired me on Friday, and that's when she told me about this assignment." She doesn't make eye contact with me, as she holds her enormous shoulder bag in front of herself and covers her neck with one hand, subconsciously protecting her most vulnerable body parts. "I wasn't sure if it was appropriate to call you on the weekend," she says to Keaton.

I'm not even aware of his reaction to this news.

The way my brain blanks out now is nothing like when I came inside of her.

I have no idea what's going on right now. All I know is that the bandage that I was planning on ripping off for Keaton is staying exactly where it is, and Aimee just ripped apart my fucking heart.

CHAPTER 11
AIMEE

The Mother of all Mondays has turned out to be one stressful ass ache of a motherfucker so far.

I had nodded off in the wee small hours of the morning, still warm and damp from hot shower sex with Chase and woken up by myself in a dark room thinking it was still somewhere within the realm of nighttime. It wasn't. It was just after eight o'clock. I called out to Chase, and when he didn't answer, I started to panic. When I opened the curtains and read the note that he'd left me, I really panicked.

Morning, angel.

I didn't want to wake you because you seem to be sound asleep, and you didn't mention having any appointments today. The room is paid for. Order anything you want from room service and stay until noon if you'd like. I'll tell them not to disturb you.

Thank you for the night of my life.

I will be in touch as soon as I get my phone back.

I want to see you again tonight, and the next night, and the next.

I have decided to tell Keaton about us. Sooner rather than later.

See you soon.

--Chase

P.S. I'd say we burned everything down to the ground last night, wouldn't you?

I could not believe he left without waking me up first. I was going to tell him about my job when we woke up. It's on me. I know that's on me, but *mother of balls*, I did not want to lose our night together. It never would have occurred to me that he wouldn't wake me up before leaving! Now I felt like I was going to lose that hot dog I'd eaten last night on the hotel room floor. I did not have time to order room service. I did not have time to shower again or charge my phone or deal with my chaotic hair. I barely had time to get dressed so I could run out the door and get a cab home to change clothes.

While I was in the cab I tried calling Chase every single minute, but it went straight to voicemail every time. I knew full well that if he tells Keaton about us before I show up for our meeting it will be a nightmare and I'll probably be fired right out of the gate.

Roxy was home, already dressed and ready to go to work. I didn't even have the time or words to explain to her what the problem was, and I didn't have to. She took one look at me, nodded once, and said, "Well, at least you got laid. Don't worry, I can cover rent next month." Then she tossed a bagel at me while I was running out the door.

Now I'm standing here in front of the man I rejected last week and the man I fellated in the shower last night, and neither of them have anything to say to me after being informed of my new position as their project manager. I finally manage to look at Chase, and it feels like someone is dumping ice water on me. His jaw is clenched, his fists are clenched, his whole body is just clenched. If looks could kill, I'd be a dead woman. But it really kills me to see him struggling to comprehend this while maintaining his composure. I didn't want to have to tell him like this.

It's a good thing that he hasn't told Keaton about us yet, but when it comes to me and Chase, I can see that I am screwed. And not in the way that I want to be.

Fine.

If he's going to prioritize his buddy and his company over me and the night we just had together, then he should understand why I am going to prioritize my new job and my indignance over his not waking me up over his anger toward me about not telling him sooner.

Just as Keaton is about to open his smirky mouth and say something that I'm fairly sure will be along the lines of: "Well, I guess it's fate, then," I hear Elaine Hoffman's voice behind me.

"Oh good, we're all here," she says.

It's still ten minutes before our meeting was supposed to start.

I clear my throat and turn to her. "Elaine, hi! You're early too, I see."

"My dad always used to say, 'If you're not ten minutes early, you're ten minutes late.' Of course, one day when he'd left for work ten minutes early, he got hit by a truck that was running late for a delivery. I still haven't figured out what the meaning of that story is, but there you go."

Keaton barks out a laugh, and then realizes that she's dead serious.

"Oh my God, Elaine, I'm so sorry." I touch her arm.

"It was years ago, and he was a dick. But we're all here, so let's rock and roll!"

"We'll sit down in the conference room over here," Chase mutters.

Elaine gives me the once-over. "Must have been windier in your neighborhood than mine this morning."

I try to pat my hair down but there is no hiding the bedhead. I look like I've been shagged six ways from Sunday, and I totally was. "I air-dried," I shrug.

"Everything good here?" she whispers, as we follow Chase and Keaton to the conference room.

"All good. How are you?"

She rolls her eyes. "Oh, you know. Monday's the new Friday. Work is my salvation."

"Mine too. I think."

I hope.

I've got my usual introductory spiel for executives down pat. Elaine is really only here as a formality.

Once we're in the conference room, Keaton offers us food and drink from the impressive spread that's set up on a console table along the wall, and Chase goes off "to grab Greg."

I take advantage of his absence to gather my wits about me and will myself to ignore the fact that I can still feel him everywhere—all over and inside of me.

I'm a pro.

I've got an MBA.

I got this.

I'll just power through this meeting, impress everyone so much that it becomes crystal clear to them that only a moron would fire me, and I will continue to do my job.

Chase brings in a very handsome Asian man, who has the most beautiful complexion I have ever seen on an adult male human.

"I'm Greg Lee, CTO," he says. "Really good to meet you."

"I'm Aimee Gilpin, hello." We shake hands, and while he greets Elaine, I stare at his face like I weirdo.

He smiles at me. "You're thinking I have nice skin, aren't you?"

"It's not just nice, it's beautiful!"

"My fiancée is an aesthetician. She has a YouTube channel and she's always experimenting with facials on me."

This is good. This is exactly the kind of casual friendly energy I need to start out this meeting. I ask him who his fiancée is, because Roxy and I have spent hours watching YouTube tutorials on how to be exceptionally gorgeous, and it turns out I know exactly who she is. He lets me touch his face and Elaine and I giggle because he's so nice and cool, and then Chase grumbles about how we should probably get on with the meeting.

He dresses for work exactly as he does when he's at a bar at night, which is not at all disappointing, but it's starting to look like CEO Chase might be an asshole. At least to me. At least for now. And a tiny rebellious part of me might be a tiny bit turned on by that.

On with the show.

I have my standard PowerPoint presentation ready on my laptop, and since there are only four other people at the table, I don't have to fuss with hooking it up to a projector or a monitor. I launch into my speech about what I've studied, where I've worked, which companies I've worked for during their transitions to a subscription-based model. I show them graphs and pie charts and conversion rates, give them a rundown of the best ways to offset initial existing customer resistance to the new format.

I make eye contact with Greg Lee seventy percent of the time. I will be working closely with him, since he is the CTO, and much of the transition involves new software and interfaces. Also, he's engaged and I don't have to worry about him either trying to date me or trying to murder me with his eyes.

When I do finally look over at Chase, though, I can see that his body language has softened.

Not in the way that it was last night—although his body wasn't exactly soft for much of the time last night.

But Business Consultant Aimee is winning over CEO Chase.

This might just work out for us, after all.

I trip up over a sentence when all of a sudden, my brain presents me with the image of his head between my legs. But I recover.

As soon as I notice the corner of his mouth tugging upwards, I look away from him. He knows what I was thinking just now and he's loving that it got to me. *Jerk.*

I'm pretty sure no one else will be suspicious as to why he and I are both grinning all of a sudden.

Before I know it, my presentation has come to a conclusion, and the key executives of SnapLegal-NYC are thanking me and saying that they look forward to working with me. Well, Greg Lee is, anyway.

Elaine tells me to stop by to see her in the afternoon because my office and new business cards will be ready, and then she rushes off to her next meeting. Greg saunters off to join a conference call, leaving me with Chase and Keaton and only a fraction of the devastating awkwardness I was feeling before the meeting.

They lead me out of the conference room and Chase asks a diminutive spitfire of a young lady named Nora to give me a tour of the office, show me to my temporary desk, and introduce me to everyone. Nora doesn't agree to do what the CEO says, she just looks at Keaton and awaits further instruction.

"Yeah, do that," Keaton says to Nora. "Chase and I are gonna have a little talk about something totally unrelated in his office. Great job, Aimee. See you in a bit."

Chase doesn't look me in the eyes, but I do catch him glancing at my bare legs and four inch heels.

They go off to what I assume is Chase's office. I feel good about this. I'm feeling good about everything. The SnapLegal offices are awesome and they're in a great building. This space is bright and open, but with enclosed offices and meeting rooms and probably a break room, along the perimeter. You can pretty much see where everyone is and what they're doing, but there's also privacy to be had if necessary. I'd say there are maybe thirteen people here, which is a good number for a company that's just under two years old.

"Aimee Gilpin?" Nora smirks. "The Aimee Gilpin who received a two hundred-dollar flower arrangement at The Mercer Group a few weeks ago?"

Well, shit. Of course. Keaton's assistant sent the flowers. Keaton's assistant knows that he was trying to woo me and probably thinks I slept with him to get this job or something.

"One and the same, yes. Unfortunately, my position there was terminated. But thank you so much for the flowers. They were so gorgeous. You have excellent taste." I consider my next words very carefully, lower my voice and say: "I hope it's not weird that I never went out with Keaton. He's such a great guy, but obviously it turns out it's a good thing that we never got involved." I try to play the girl-talk card, get her on my side, figure out if she's in love with her boss or not.

She snorts. "Yeah, whatever. He's a horndog. Let's just say you weren't the only girl I had flowers sent to this past few weeks. But yours were the second-most expensive … I'm not sure where they were planning on putting you. There's a free desk over on Chase's side and there's one right here by Keaton and me."

"It's usually good for me to be within earshot of the CEO," I find myself blurting out.

"Uh huh." Nora smirks again. "That makes sense."

I can't tell if Nora is going to be an ally or an enemy, but I definitely need to stay on her good side. Find out her favorite coffee place and bring her a latte and a croissant tomorrow.

As she leads the way toward the staff that she's going to introduce me to, I can't help glancing over at Chase's office. The dividing wall is tempered glass, frosted to about five feet up from the ground so that you can't see him when he's seated. All I see is Keaton pacing around, gesticulating, and rubbing his forehead.

Well, shit.

I suppose there is a chance that they are actually discussing a totally unrelated matter, but it's more likely that Roxy will indeed have to pay next month's rent.

CHAPTER 12
CHASE

Keaton is pacing back and forth in front of my desk and I want to kill him. It is so messed up that I have to manage *his* response to this situation, when I need to be dealing with my own. If Aimee weren't so fucking awesome when she gave that little presentation, I would have tried to find a way to get out of our contract with Elaine. But she rocked it. I have a whole new level of attraction to her. And I can't do a fucking thing about it for now.

"Fuuuuuck … she's hot. She looks hotter today than before she shot me down. Am I crazy?"

"Yes."

"Yes I'm crazy or yes she does look hotter than she did before she shot me down?"

"It's not an either-or situation."

"She definitely looks hotter now than she did before I slept with Quinn. That's not good. Maybe Aimee showing up here is a sign that I should keep trying with her, right? I mean what are the chances? This is the fucking universe telling me that she's the one I should be with. That I shouldn't give up."

I think the fucking universe might be telling me it's time I knock some sense into my best friend and CFO, but fuck the universe. It's not doing me any favors today, that's all I know.

"You need to lower your voice and watch your fucking mouth around the office."

"What's up your ass?"

"What's up yours? Did it not go well in the Hamptons?"

"I mean … It went well. First times and all that. Quinn's gorgeous and hot. Right? When my dad found out I was going to the Hamptons with her he actually said, 'good for you.' You know how many times he's said that to me? Twice. Once when I sold that lot in Queens for a million-dollar profit and once when he found out I'm dating Quinn Parker."

"Then keep it going with Quinn."

Even while he's nodding his head, he says, "Shit. What if I made a mistake?"

"Can you be a fucking CFO for five minutes and focus on the matter at hand?"

"That's all I'm focusing on! How do you not have even the slightest bit of empathy for me in this scenario?"

"Trust me, I can empathize with you. I just don't have any sympathy for you."

"We need to get out of this contract."

"Don't be such a selfish asshole—think about the optics. Think about what that would do to Aimee if her boss finds out you don't want to work with her—she'd probably get fired on her first day. Did you not pay attention to a word she said in that meeting? She knows her shit and we don't have time to find another consultant for this. We have to stick to our schedule. She's only going to be working in our office for one month. Just nut up and pull it together. It'll be over before we know it."

"You're right. You're right. This way I can feel things out with her here while I decide if things are working out with Quinn."

I don't know if I'm literally turning red and if steam is actually shooting out of my ears right now, but it sure as fuck feels like it.

"Yeah. I'm too tired to get up and punch you in the head right now. You will feel no one out at work. You had your shot with Aimee and she turned you down. You've moved on. Remember? Jesus. What is wrong with you?"

"I don't know. I didn't get any sleep all weekend."

"Neither did I, but at least I can think with my brain instead of my dick."

"Why didn't you get any sleep?"

"The usual reasons. This isn't about me—this is about *you* thinking like the CFO of this company and not like some adolescent prick."

He finally takes a breath and half-smiles. "It's not an either-or situation."

There he is. "You good now?"

He nods and rubs his face. I've never seen him this stressed-out and worked-up before. He must have had a really bad time with Quinn on the weekend. Either that, or he really has a thing for Aimee.

"How about this … You don't even have to work with her directly. You don't need to be in the meetings. She can deal with me and Greg when she has to talk to the executive team, she can write up reports for you and send them to me. I will then forward to you. We won't let anyone else know about this arrangement. We'll tell Tyler that as VP of Sales he is point on this project, but this is what it will take for you to stay on the right path with Quinn. And you *know* the smart thing to do is stay on the right path with Quinn. Right?"

Okay, I'll admit it. I'm being a selfish, manipulative dick. But Keaton wants Quinn because his parents will approve—not just approve—they'll actually have some respect for him for a change.

He looks relieved. I, however, am unsure of who will actually benefit from this solution. I just know that I do not want Keaton and Aimee alone in a room together. For business reasons.

"That's a good idea. Thanks, man. Sorry, I know I'm being a shithead. I hope Aimee understands."

"I'll make sure that she does."

I think he'll be okay, if he just stays focused on his job and Quinn. Keaton usually has great instincts when it comes to investments, when it comes to tracking cash flow, analyzing financial strengths and weaknesses, courting investors and clients, sweet-talking our board members. But when it comes to making choices in his personal life, Keaton is—how shall I put this? He's a fucking idiot.

Honestly, the smartest thing he's ever done, when it comes to love interests, was to pursue Aimee. And I don't know yet if not telling him about what happened between me and Aimee last night is the dumbest thing I'll ever do, but I know I can't tell him now and I know that if I ever see him lay a hand on her, I will eviscerate him.

"Just go easy on her," he says. "I know she's not your favorite person."

"What do you mean?"

"You're always such a dick whenever I bring her up."

"That's because you never shut up about her. I am not a dick to the people I work with."

Keaton looks down at the Breitling that his mom gave him for his birthday last year and sighs. "I've got a conference call in a few minutes. See you later."

"Close the door behind you, will ya?"

He straightens up, tugs on his shirt sleeves, and steels himself before walking out of my office, shutting the door.

As soon as he's gone, I slouch down in my chair, cover my face and do a silent scream. The agony I'll be experiencing from now on is all on me, I know that. Would I have done things differently last night if Aimee had come clean as soon as she got to the bar?

Probably not.

Am I still pissed that she never mentioned it?

Very.

Does it change the way I feel about her?

Not even a little bit.

Did I honestly think it would be easy dealing with the Keaton of it all?

No.

But there is no way she and I can be together the way I want to be with her while she's working here. I'm looking at another month of torture on a whole new level.

I sit up to have a peek at what's going on outside my office. I'm really wishing we'd leased one of those old-school office spaces with a bunch of private rooms and hallways instead of this beautiful open design shit where everyone can see everything. Nora is leading Aimee over to the empty desk nearby. It's better than having her close to Keaton, and I do need to have her around in case I need her to get on my calls with existing clients about the transition, but ... this is gonna hurt. On so many levels.

When Nora hustles off to get Keaton on his conference call, I step out of my office. Aimee is getting comfortable at her new desk, setting up her laptop. She must be completely aware that I'm standing here, three feet away from her, but she's refusing to look over at me. Now she's pulling out her phone, a notebook and pens, and placing them, very precisely and loudly, on the desktop. Finally, she becomes very still and sighs.

"Got everything you need here?"

"Getting what I deserve, apparently," she mutters. "Should I even bother getting settled in?" She gives me a hesitant sidelong glance that tears me apart inside.

"Your job is safe," I say. "We'll talk more in a bit." I tap my fingers on the desktop and drop a folded-up note there, then walk out to the stairwell without making eye contact with anyone.

I used to come up here alone to the roof deck for a cigarette once a day. This is the first time I've been up here in a month. There's no patio furniture, but there's a great view. Since we're the tallest building in the area, there's the illusion of privacy.

I feel like a fucking schoolboy under the bleachers waiting for Aimee to show up. In the note, I told her to meet me here in five minutes so we can talk. It has now been seven minutes and I'm ready to jump. I hate not having my phone. And now I'm finally realizing that it's a quarter to ten and I haven't even started responding to emails or voice messages yet. This had been such a boring, drama-free workplace until today.

The heavy metal door opens a crack, and my new favorite face pokes out from behind it. I can tell she has no idea what to expect from me. I can tell that I can trust her to be professional. For the first time ever, I just don't know if I can trust myself.

She stands by the closed door, arms crossed in front of her chest. "Sorry I'm late."

I stay where I am, about five feet from her. My crossed arms mirror hers. She keeps her stare fixed on them, instead of my eyes.

"I've discussed this with Keaton, and I think the best way to go about this is for you to limit your interactions with him as much as possible. Aside from the tech department and me, you'll primarily be dealing with

Tyler, the VP of Sales on this. Anything regarding this project that's finance-related can be written up in a report and sent to me, and I'll forward it to Keaton. Don't include him in your Slack messages when you set up your channels. If you have any questions for him, I also want you to tell me and I will relay them to him."

Instead of commenting on how extreme that sounds, she merely nods her head. "Is he going to be okay with this?"

"He'll be fine. Just don't flirt with him."

"I've never flirted with him!" she snaps.

"Great, then keep it up. Don't make it obvious that you're trying to avoid him or anything."

She huffs. "Believe it or not, Keaton isn't the first person that I've worked with who's asked me out. I have become rather adept at handling myself around men in office situations."

"He isn't the first 'person' you've worked with to ask you out?" I can't help myself. "You're saying that women have asked you out too?"

"Does that surprise you?"

And that's just one more thing to add to the list of things that I can't allow myself to think about for a month.

"I don't know if you've figured it out for yourself or not yet, but Keaton's assistant Nora knows a lot about his personal business, so …"

"Yeah. I know. She had flowers sent to my old office. I don't think she'll be an issue."

I cringe at the memory of Keaton trying to date her. In a way, it feels like it was so long ago.

"Just don't mention anything to her about us,

because she gets bored easily and she'll tell Keaton just for shits and giggles."

She frowns at me. "*Us?* What exactly do you mean by that?"

"Last night, I mean. Obviously, we can't see each other outside of work while you're here, and there can be no hint of intimate behavior at the office."

"Yeah. I get it. I am not an idiot."

"No, you're not. But you must think I am."

Suddenly, her deep blue eyes look wet. She takes a step toward me and jabs at the air. "I tried to get ahold of you all day yesterday and I went to Bitters last night because I wanted to tell you about my job and ask you how to handle it!" Her sudden rage is all it takes to unhinge me.

I take a step forward too. "And then you got there and all of a sudden—what—you forgot?!"

"No, I made a decision! I decided to tell you first thing in the morning instead, but you just left me there in the hotel room like a prostitute!"

"I am truly sorry if that made you feel like a prostitute, but I was under the impression that you were unemployed, and I wanted to let you sleep. How was I supposed to know you had a meeting with me in my office?"

"I would have told you if it weren't so much more important to you to run off to talk to Keaton instead of saying 'good morning' to me after a night of fucking!" She lunges towards me and shoves me.

I grab her wrists and hold them in front of me. "That's not all last night was to me and you know it!"

"How? How would I know it? From your little note?!"

"Do not confuse me being rational about this with me not caring about you."

"Hah! Don't confuse my anger with me needing you to care about me, Chase. It was just one night." Her voice is strained, and I can feel her shaking. Not even trying to pull away from me, she just stands there, inches from me, glaring at me.

Goddammit. Those wild, deep blue eyes are driving me insane.

Letting go of her wrists, I grab her face and kiss her hard, running my fingers through her crazy hair. She responds with moans and hands all over me, sighing and saying my name over and over in that way that makes me feel completely powerful and totally at her mercy. If she weren't in that tight fucking skirt that shows every hot curve, I'd have her legs wrapped around my waist by now, but I back her up until she's against the door. She has all of the urgency that she had last night after the roller coaster plus the added energy of an enraged cat, alternately swiping and clutching at me while I kiss her neck.

"Don't ever leave me like that again," she says, her voice hoarse.

"I won't."

She tugs on my earlobe with her teeth. "You better not."

The sound of a helicopter flying overhead suddenly wakes me up and reminds me where we are and what time it is and who we are and who we can't be to each other right now.

I untangle myself from her and step away.

She gasps and swears under her breath, looking at me with a mix of resentment, lust, apology, forgiveness and confusion.

We both straighten ourselves up and clear our throats.

"That can't happen again," I say, finding my CEO voice.

"It won't."

She finishes tucking in her blouse. I readjust my throbbing angry dick, and then we both wipe our mouths with the backs of our hands.

"Thanks for not wearing lipstick," I say.

After a beat, we both laugh.

"This is going to suck. I was so ready to tell Keaton about us, because I want to be with you, anytime we want, but we just can't while you're working here."

She looks down at her shoes. "I know. Personally, I find it helps to remember that one day we're all going to be dead. And that will be so much better than this." She twists her lips to one side.

God, she's adorable.

"I really did love our night together."

She nods while combing her fingers through her hair and says, voice barely above a whisper: "I can still feel you inside of me."

I brush her hair out of her eyes. It's a mistake. The second I touch her I just want more again. Taking her face in my hands, I lower my lips to hers.

Instead of kissing me back, she says, "I have to go call my mom back and then talk with your employees." Then, in an inexplicably sexy move, she reaches inside her blouse, further down inside her bra, and pulls out a small card, which she presses into the palm of my hand.

Then she sidesteps away from me, opens the door and disappears, leaving me alone again with the fresh air and a boner and a feeling of confusion and dread.

I look down at the card, which I had assumed is her new business card, but it's the fortune card she got from the Zoltar machine at Luna Park last night, which reads:

"You may be riding the winds of change. Things may at times seem to be out of touch. Soon they will come down to a better order."

She is so fucking sweet and I am so fucking mad about this mess.

I picked a bad time to quit smoking.

CHAPTER 13
AIMEE

'␣ve learned a lot in the past week.

I've learned that Chase McKay is a beautiful, sexy and skilled lover. I've learned that he's an excellent CEO who's engaged in the whole process of being a founder at SnapLegal-NYC, even down to managing their Twitter account. He understands the needs of his customers, he's a walking encyclopedia of entrepreneurship and corporate law, as well as Brooklyn history. He is an excellent leader, an upstanding member of the community, genuinely passionate about helping local brick and mortar businesses to thrive.

I've learned that he is a stubborn ass, and it's driving me crazy. He is a wise, thoughtful yet quick decision-maker, and one of the decisions he's made is to remain professional and emotionally distant from me while I'm working at his offices, despite my undeniable sexy awesomeness. It's a good business decision, but I still hate it. He listens to me and compliments and thanks me for my work when we're in the presence of other people, and I appreciate that. I respect and admire his loyalty to Keaton, dedication to his company, and ability to compartmentalize.

His resistance is so frustrating. I resent that he is so totally capable of *not* grabbing and kissing me again even just once dammit. I've learned how to work along-side him without having Wet Panty Face, despite secretly enjoying multiple micro-orgasms while staring at his hands and remembering all of the devastating things they did to me.

To sum up: Chase McKay seems to be handling our current situation with a certain kind of masculine grace, flair and ease, while I am a big, horny, functional mess.

I've been in a near-constant state of arousal since meeting that man over a month ago. But no matter how completely, blissfully satisfied I was for one night, I am far more frustrated now than I was for the month that led up to that night.

After a weekend spent cleaning and reorganizing every single thing in this apartment and nearly wear-ing-out my vibrator, I have been calmly observing how interesting it is that Chase has opted to refrain from contacting me at all. This is why Roxy is currently advising me to: "Get your tits out, baby, this is war."

She's laying out "a fuck you outfit" on my bed—an outfit that I would never even wear on a date, much less to work on a Monday morning. She thinks my only option is to "give Chase blue balls until his dick falls off from lack of oxygen." Which is probably not how it would work, physiologically-speaking, but I get her point. I just don't want anything bad to happen to Chase's dick or to his balls. As much as I hate how stubborn he's being, I still like all of his body parts, and his face, and hair. I even like his brain, I just don't understand it.

In lieu of the bustier, blazer and spandex mini-skirt that Roxy has selected, I've decided to wear my Halloween costume from two years ago, when I went as Joan Cusack from *Working Girl.* Minus the hairspray, eye make-up and shoulder pads. I rocked that office Halloween party, but I don't want to get laughed out of SnapLegal.

Roxy crosses her arms as she stands back to take me in, in all of my brown and burnt orange, shapeless glory. "Right. So, your plan is to be so unattractive that his dick shrivels up? That's original."

"No, my plan is to be one hundred percent professional, if that's what Chase wants. If he doesn't want to acknowledge that we had sex multiple times, then I'm not going to acknowledge that I am a sexual being."

Roxy does an admirable job of not laughing at me. "Uh huh. Well, as long as you're owning it. *You go, girl!* You have a head for business and a bod for eating your lunch in a toilet stall while crying."

"I'm feeling really good about my decision, so don't try to stop me from walking out the door looking like this."

"Oh, I'm not going to. I can't wait to read your freelance story about this on Bustle!"

. . .

I can't believe she let me leave the house looking like this. I can't believe I didn't bring an alternative outfit for when I realize what a dumb idea this was. However, I can now say for certain that Sigourney Weaver's advice to Melanie Griffith in *Working Girl* was brilliant: "Dress shabbily and they notice the dress. Dress impeccably and they notice the woman." I manage to hold my head up high as I greet everyone during my walk of wardrobe shame, from the entrance to SnapLegal, all the way to my desk. But when I see Chase through the open door to his office, I want to die.

Instead of his usual T-shirt and jeans look, which is still somehow impossibly sexy and appropriate in all situations, he is wearing a white button-down shirt under a dark suit. He must have a lunch or dinner appointment somewhere fancy. His shirt is casually unbuttoned to a point where I can see the top of the tattoo below his clavicle, and he looks so sexy I want to stab myself in the eyes with the pen I'm gripping so I don't have to look at him.

Whose idea was it to wear dowdy clothes on the day he decides to suit up?

He's talking on his office phone while leaning against the back of his desk, and when he sees me, he signals to me to join him. He continues talking on the phone, while looking me up and down. If his dick is shriveling up, I can't tell, because he's so good at talking to people on the phone in a way that makes them feel like he's actually giving them his full attention.

"Caleb, let me grab my project manager so we can

get her on the phone with you. She's a lot better at explaining this stuff than I am. Can I put you on hold for a second? Thanks." He presses the 'hold' button and presses the phone to his chest. "I've got an important customer here. He was one of the first when we launched. I sent out the email you helped me draft last week—"

"Yeah, you bcc'd me."

"And he has some concerns about the upcoming changes."

"Shouldn't your VP of Sales be dealing with this?"

"I deal with the VIPs directly. Can you give him your pitch?"

"Lemme at him."

He smirks. "Have a seat," he says, as he goes around to his own chair.

I take a seat in front of his desk and clear my throat. In the next five minutes, I proceed to give Mr. VIP my patented "this is why subscription services are better for everyone and here's what we're going to offer you as a special bonus for being one of the first to sign up" pitch on speakerphone. Chase leans back and watches me, chimes in only when necessary. By the time we hang up, Caleb can't even wait to switch from on demand à la carte member to annual subscriber of SnapLegal-NYC's services.

I remain seated and we stare at each other, for what feels like an eternity. He smells so fucking good I just want to rub my face against his sweat glands for half an hour or so—is that too much to ask?

"Thank you," he finally says. "That was great."

"It's what I'm here for."

He nods. "You have a good weekend?"

"Yes!" I practically yell out. "Great! You?!"

"I was here working most of the time."

"Oh." *Shit, I should have come to the office.* "You work on weekends a lot?"

"More often than not."

"You going someplace nice later or something?"

"Lunch with a board member," he says reassuringly. Like he knows I'm worried he's got a date or something. "Thanks again," he says, turning his attention to his laptop.

I guess that's my cue to leave. "Right. Well, let me know if you get any more calls or emails that you want me to handle."

"Will do."

When I get to the door, he says, "By the way, if you're wearing that outfit because you were trying to make yourself less attractive to me, I appreciate it, but you'll have to try harder." I look back at him. He doesn't even look up from his laptop. Is he flirting with me? I can't tell.

"If you were trying to look so sexy that I'd throw myself at you, you'll have to try harder."

He still doesn't look up from his laptop. "Duly noted," he says, and then he picks up his office phone. "Would you mind closing the door behind you? Thanks."

When I get back to my desk, I check my personal phone and find a text from FOXY ROXY: *How's that boner-reducing outfit working out for you so far today?*

I respond with: *<shrugging woman emoji> <eggplant emoji> <Swiss Flag emoji>*

FOXY ROXY: *Huh?!?!*

ME: *Neutral eggplant. No idea what's going on with him. Thanks for letting me dress like this in public, btw. <devil face emoji> <skull and crossbones emoji>*

FOXY ROXY: *It hurts me as much as it hurts you ... and the eyeballs of everyone who has to see you today. <blowing kisses emoji>*

FOXY ROXY: *This is how we learn, babycakes. Tomorrow is another day.*

CHAPTER 14
AIMEE

I wake up ten minutes before my alarm on Tuesday morning, because I'm so excited to get dressed. I'm not going to wear Roxy's office porno outfit, but I am going to wear her second-string suggestion: the red Diane Von Furstenberg wrap dress that a former colleague in Ann Arbor once very inappropriately referred to as being "just mean to people with penises who are trying to work over here." I beg to differ. If Diane Von Furstenberg designed it, then it is perfectly suited for day-to-night business lady apparel. Even though my only plans for tonight involve typing up reports and figuring out what I'm going to wear for an encore tomorrow.

When Roxy walks out of the bathroom and sees me, she says, "Now *that's* what I'm talking about."

I try to ignore my gut reaction—which is to do the opposite of anything Roxy would approve of—and respond to her high-five.

"That'll put a tingle in his dongle."

"I mean. If he doesn't want to date me, then I'll have to move on and find someone who does. Right?"

"You don't actually believe he doesn't want to date you?"

"You don't actually believe he does, do you?"

She shakes her head and rolls her eyes. "First of all, you look so hot in that dress I think *I* might want to date you. Secondly, it's like you need to be hit over the head with an erect penis before you understand how a guy feels about you. He never told you he doesn't want to date you, dummy! If he didn't really care about a future with you, he wouldn't be trying so hard to keep his hands off of you when that other guy's around."

"Then why doesn't he want to see me at night or on the weekends?"

"Because that would make it even harder for him to keep his hands off of you at the office."

"I thought you wanted me to give him blue balls."

"I do. I'm not saying I approve of his behavior; I'm just saying I understand it. It's like when you're trying to do a juice cleanse. You can't lick the junk food in between juices to keep from eating it, cuz if you lick a potato chip you're gonna eat that whole bag of chips. Just go to work with the same attitude you had yesterday, only not in an outfit that makes people want to vomit."

I hate it when I realize this woman is, in fact, more rational than I am. I hate it every single time I realize it. And now all I want to do is lick Chase McKay and eat a bag of potato chips.

"It's only three more weeks," she continues. "Less

than that. Even I can keep it in my pants around a guy I'm attracted to for that long."

Before I can laugh in her face and demand examples, I have to answer a call from my mom. I've been talking her through a minor annoyance that has been slowly becoming a minor crisis. Apparently, no one in the Gilpin family is good at dealing with problems head-on lately.

By the time I get to the office, I've been ogled countless times, whistled at twice, and offered one marriage proposal from a construction worker. I'm feeling pretty good about things, until I catch sight of Chase McKay.

Today, he's wearing a button-down shirt, classic-fit vest, blazer and belted trousers, with beautiful cognac leather Oxford shoes. His hair is up in a loose man bun and he's wearing glasses. It actually feels like I've been punched in the heart. He looks like a cover model for Professor Man Bun Quarterly. I don't know if that's a real magazine, but if it is, sign me up.

He's standing next to Greg Lee, reading something on the iPad that Greg's holding up for him. When he sees me staring at him, he grins. I guess he took my suggestion to try harder to look so sexy that I'd throw myself at him. I also think he may be trying to kill me.

Lady blue balls are real.

My poor parents will have to explain to people that their daughter passed away after her vulva exploded in a freak workplace accident.

I wonder if my life insurance covers that.

Keaton isn't in his office when I pass by, but Nora is watching me like a hawk. She might have seen me eye-boning Chase *McNotOkayToDressLikeThatUnlessYouFuck-MeDammit*. She gives me a little nod, like she knows what's up. She doesn't know what's up. I give her a casual wave and keep walking.

Almost as soon as I've signed into Slack—the team messaging software that they use here—I receive a direct message from Tyler, the VP of Sales. I've been working with him quite closely on this project, and I get about twenty direct messages from him a day, and even more on the group channels. Tyler is very single, incredibly flirtatious, and totally harmless. I think. He's so flirtatious that surely no woman can take him seriously.

TYLER: *Gooood morning, Red Dress! I'm so flattered that you dressed-up for my b-day. You and that dress better be here for my lunch party later. <raising hands emoji>*

I forgot about the birthday lunch party, but if Tyler wants to think I dressed-up for him, so be it.

AIMEE: *Happy birthday to you! My dress and I have every intention of attending your lunch party. <dancing lady in red dress emoji>.*

AIMEE: *I'll have that report on flexible subscription pricing and distinct offerings to you tomorrow morning, FYI*

TYLER: *As long as that distinctive red dress is part of the offer!*

AIMEE: *Get back to work, Tyler <angel face emoji>*

. . .

Seconds later, I get a text on my personal phone, from Keaton. I look up and see that he's in his office, looking out at me. He walks away from his window as soon as I see him. This is the first time he's texted me since the day I told him I didn't want to date him.

KEATON: *Hey, I'm hearing nothing but great things about your work here, FYI. You gonna be here for the birthday lunch thing later? It's someone's birthday, idk who, I'm just paying for it.*

Well, that's a fairly harmless text, I suppose.

ME: *Hey, thank you so much for telling me that! I'm really enjoying it here, you guys have a great company. Yes, I will be here for Tyler's party.*

KEATON: *<thumbs-up emoji>*

Still within the bounds of propriety.

KEATON: *<winking face emoticon>*

Ahh, the winking face emoticon. Always a difficult one to read when received from a straight man. I don't respond.

My Slack app alerts me that I've received a direct message from Chase. Just seeing his face on the tiny icon gives me shameless butterflies.

CHASE: *I followed up with all of the customers we spoke with yesterday, btw. All good. Thx again for your help with that.*

AIMEE: *My pleasure! It's what I'm here for.*

I'm certainly not here for you to bend me over your desk

or take me back up to the roof deck and make out with me again. Unfortunately.

As soon as I've sent my response, I receive a message from him on one of the group channels, regarding customer support.

I reply immediately, drag and drop my generic report on the subject, and several others join in on the conversation with questions for me.

Meanwhile, I receive a text from Chase McKay on my personal cell phone. It's the first time he's ever sent me a text from his personal phone. I stop what I'm typing on my laptop so I can read it.

CHASE MCKAY: *Nice dress. In case you're wondering, you're still going to have to work a little harder to make yourself unattractive to me.*

No ellipses. No emojis. Just *that.*

Lifting my ass up from my chair, I check to see if he's even looking at me from his office. He isn't. I can see the top of his man bun. He appears to be talking on his office phone.

I text him back, knowing that if he had any idea his text came in after one from Keaton, he would stop texting me immediately.

ME: *Nice <u>everything</u>. But in case you haven't noticed, I still haven't thrown myself at you yet.*

Shit! I hit send before realizing I shouldn't have typed the word "yet."

CHASE MCKAY: *"Yet?"*

ME: *That was a typo. I meant "yep." As in: Yep, that's right. Still not throwing myself at you.*

I look up at my laptop screen and see that Chase has

sent me another message on a group Slack channel, about marketing.

I respond with another question.

He sends back a Slack message that says: *Yep.*

I get an iMessage from Foxy Roxy and open up my Messages app on my laptop so I don't look like I'm constantly texting on my phone. Fortunately, there's no one seated behind me at this office.

FOXY ROXY: *How many penis dragons has the red dress slayed so far?*

AIMEE: *I AM NEVER TAKING YOUR ADVICE ABOUT ANYTHING! EVER AGAIN! I MEAN EVER!!!*

TYLER: *Whoa! Calm down, Red Dress! Who was that directed at?*

GREG: *If a woman is yelling, she's yelling at you, @Tyler.*

JULIA: *Word. Although, @Chase does give pretty bad advice about work/life balance.*

CHASE: *Yep.*

AIMEE: *I am so sorry, you guys! That message was meant for someone else. <blushing face emoji>*

TYLER: *Aww, her emoji matches her dress today.*

CHASE: *Get back to work, Tyler.*

TYLER: *<raising hands emoji> <angel face emoji>*

I get a text from Chase McKay on my phone.

CHASE MCKAY: *Let me guess. Roxy dressed you again today.*

ME: *You don't know me!*

ME: *I'm really never taking her advice on anything ever again ever, though.*

CHASE MCKAY: *And I'm still a big fan of her work.*

I look up when his door opens. He walks out and over to Greg's office, without glancing over at me. He's just grinning and shaking his head.

Yep. He's trying to kill me.

Once again, I should have brought an alternate outfit. It's not even lunch yet, and this red dress is wearing me out. I was a lot more productive yesterday.

CHAPTER 15
CHASE

I've learned a lot in the past week.

I've learned that Aimee Gilpin is hot as hell, and I have to fight every urge to rip her clothes off, even when she's dressed like my nonna. I've learned that refraining from saying or doing the things that I desperately want to say and do to her does absolutely nothing to curb my intense physical attraction to her, but I've become a world class champion at hiding it.

I've learned that she's one of the best and most reliable business consultants I've ever met, and despite the very unprofessional circumstances we've found ourselves in, she is every bit the professional we need her to be. I've learned that if I stay at the office after she's gone, I can still smell her when I walk past her desk, and I am an asshole for sitting at her desk over the weekend while thinking about our night together and stubbornly refusing to call her.

I've learned that seeing her in a red dress is just as arousing as seeing her naked and knowing that other men are seeing her in that dress right now makes my blood boil.

The catering that I ordered from Tyler's restaurant of choice is set up in the center of our office, and he's already suckered Aimee into singing *"You're the One That I Want"* with him on the karaoke machine. I need another drink. I may have to break my "one beer per person" rule for this lunch party. I may have to break the karaoke machine. And I may have to fire Tyler.

Keaton brings his sushi plate over to sit next to me. With his wide eyes staring at me, I know exactly what he's thinking: "Fuck me, how am I supposed to stay away from that woman?"

I pat him on the knee. *I don't know, just stay the fuck away from her, my friend, so I don't have to punch you.*

"How's it going with Quinn?" I ask, as if it's easy to maintain a conversation while Tyler's doing a shitty John Travolta imitation and Aimee's being sexy in a completely adorable way twenty feet from us.

"Good! Great. She wants to meet you."

"Yeah? She met your parents yet?"

"Not yet. Dinner at Per Se soon."

"Good. Glad to hear it."

He sighs. "Having to cross the bridge five times a week is a pain in the ass."

"You thinking of moving back to Manhattan?"

"No." He shifts around in his seat. "Maybe." He drops his tuna roll back onto the plate. "Where's this sushi from? It's sub-par."

"KanaHashi. They're clients. We love them. You don't like anyone's takeout."

"I like your mom's takeout."

"That's because she gives you free panna cotta."

"We should only order from your mom for these things."

Neither of us has taken our eyes off of Aimee this whole time.

"The sight of Aimee holding a microphone up to her mouth while absentmindedly licking her lips is what finally killed him," is what they'll carve into my tombstone.

Keaton groans, quietly, and lowers his voice. "I only want her because I can't have her, right?"

"Without a doubt."

"I think I'll go grab a bite somewhere else. Is that rude?"

"Nawww. If anything, everyone will be glad you spared them your Jay-Z impression."

"I get no respect around here," he says as he stands up.

I tear my eyes away from Aimee one second too late. He catches me gazing at her, and frowns. He gets that flash in his eyes, the one I first saw back at Wharton when he started to suspect that his girlfriend had a thing for me. Denial would be the wrong play here, so I shrug my shoulders and mouth the words, "red dress."

He half-smiles. "What're you gonna do?"

"Yep. Go call your girlfriend. Be back for our two-thirty meeting."

Keaton has mastered the art of leaving a party early without drawing attention to himself. Now, if I can just get that fucking birthday boy out of here, I might be able to enjoy my lunch. Mercifully, the *Grease* song ends, and I join my employees in applauding the performances.

Nora gets up to sing "Total Eclipse of the Heart," as usual, before anyone can stop her. Greg comes over to chat with me, a welcome distraction. I manage to look away from Aimee only five brief times—each time I feel her turning her attention towards me. It's perfectly clear to me that she's not interested in Tyler, and she's just as gracious and subtle in her way of handling this as she was with Keaton, but it's bugging me to see him dance around her like an idiot. He's one of the few other totally single guys here, but the only one who's shamelessly hitting on her. I hate that no one knows how I feel about her, and I hate that I'm the one who's ultimately responsible for this.

Just as Nora is wrapping up her trip down agony lane on the karaoke machine, I excuse myself from Greg and tell Julia to get the cake ready. She dashes into the break room, and I stand by the Yamaha keyboard that stays set-up in a corner 24/7 for our spontaneous office happy hours, birthday lunches, those long work days and nights that require a little tension-breaking, and weekends when I'm here alone playing Al Green to an empty room instead of serenading the woman I can't stop thinking about.

I hoot and holler when Nora finally shuts up as I take a seat at the keyboard. Not everyone has finished eating sushi yet, but it's time for Aimee to witness another one of my talents. I play the intro to "Bohemian Rhapsody" as a lead-in to "Happy Birthday," to get people's attention. Stealthily glancing over at Aimee as everyone crowds around, I notice her angrily biting her lower lip while staring at my fingers.

Trust me, Aimee, these fingers would rather be celebrating you right now.

When Julia wheels in the birthday cake on a little cart, I start singing the birthday song. I'm not saying I'm necessarily a good singer, but the McKay family has its share of Irish baritones who've had their pick of the lasses once they've taken over the pub piano. It's how my dad won my mom's heart, so the story goes. It's not like I'm trying to torture Aimee right now—it's just "Happy Birthday." I think of it more as a promissory note with a high interest rate and an unspecified maturity date.

I resist the urge to play "No Scrubs" by TLC after Tyler blows out the candles, because he didn't try to hide that he was wishing for Aimee. Instead, I get up and stand between them when Tyler's cutting and passing out the cake.

"Mmm, you know what would go great with this?" Tyler says. "An espresso."

Aimee sticks her tongue out and makes a face, much like she did the first time she tried Irish whiskey. "Blech!" she says. "I hate espresso."

"Aw come on! You just haven't had a good one. I should take you to Seven Point, on Washington. Australian-style espresso. So good."

I snort. "Please. All due respect to Aussies, but if it ain't done Italian-style, it ain't espresso."

"Still," Tyler says, "it's a cute location. You'd like it."

"I'll definitely check it out if I'm ever in the mood

for something incredibly bitter that sticks to my tongue and makes me gag," Aimee mutters.

While Tyler is still recovering from the mental image of her gagging on something bitter, I grab Aimee's arm and drag her sweet body into the break room. "Somebody needs to set you straight," I grumble. This is who I am now—the guy who grumbles and yanks her away from other dudes. She allows me to pull her, but as soon as we're inside the only room in our unit that actually has four walls and a door that you can't see through, she releases herself from my grasp.

I don't bother to look back, because I know she's scowling and frustrated with me. If I see that pouty mouth, I will make a very bad executive decision right here on the counter. I roll up my sleeves and start working the espresso machine and slamming espresso glasses like a boss. Like a jealous, possessive, sexually frustrated boss. I *am* the near-boiling water being forced over that ground coffee at nine times the normal amount of atmospheric pressure.

"What are you doing?" she asks, her hushed voice is deep and raspy, like after she's come five times. She doesn't sound angry, just genuinely confused.

"Pulling you a shot of espresso. I overheard you talking to your mom earlier. Everything alright?"

"Yes. Well, not exactly. She's got sort of a stressful situation brewing. Nothing dangerous or anything. But it will be fine."

"Yeah?"

"Yeah." She is quiet for a few seconds. "You can't do this. You can't ignore me and not call me and then flirt with me whenever you feel like it and drag me off like a caveman when your employees are being friendly with me and then ask me about my mom."

"Oh yeah? How *should* we deal with this? What are your suggestions? You want me to take you up to the roof deck and fuck you on our lunch break and then pretend I barely know you when we're in the office surrounded by all of my employees and my best friend who's still hung up on you?"

"Yes!"

"Beautiful, I want that too, believe me. But I know I won't be able to hide anything if we play it like that, and neither will you."

"Well, you're doing an awfully good job of acting like nothing ever happened between us."

"Am I? Because I'm doing a really shitty job of thinking about anything *but* what happened between us last Sunday. Like what you said to me at the bar, and holding your hand while we walked through Luna Park, and making you come on the beach and the way you made those kids who just got engaged feel like a royal couple even though they were total strangers, and what you did to me in the shower at the hotel, and how fucking beautiful you looked when you were sleeping. That was then. This is now. One day, if we survive this, we'll be able to do all of that again anytime we want to. Just. Not. Now."

I grab a bottle of sparkling water from the fridge, twist it open and hand it to her. "Take a sip of this to cleanse the palate."

She furrows her brow, but does as I say, then hands the bottle back to me.

I pull the espresso directly into two glasses and then give one to her, with a little spoon. "Smell it, stir it quickly, take a sip. Savor the *crema*. Let it coat your tongue."

Her eyes are wet, and she doesn't stop staring at me while stirring and then taking a sip. I lean against the counter, watching her. When she closes her eyes and licks the *crema* from her lips with her tongue, I know she gets it.

"Gawd, that's good. It's not bitter."

"No. It's complicated. But worth the trouble."

She scoffs. "We'll see about that."

I don't know if she's talking about the espresso or me or both, and I don't care. I just want to watch her lick her lips for about an hour and then go back to work. She gulps down the rest of it. She makes a sour face and sticks her tongue out, just like the first time she tried my whiskey. And then she laughs. God, I love that laugh.

"It'll be worth it. I promise," I say, reaching out to push her hair from her face.

She jerks back. "Don't touch me unless you're really going to touch me."

For one hot second, I consider *really* touching her, until I hear someone clear their throat, and Aimee and I both freeze.

Nora is standing in the doorway, a huge grin on her face, like it's *her* birthday and she just unwrapped a life-size edible Channing Tatum doll.

"How long have you been standing there?" I snap.

"I just walked in," she says, completely unable to stop grinning.

I don't believe her, but it also doesn't matter how long she's been there, because no matter what she heard or saw, it was too much.

CHAPTER 16
CHASE

Since the break room incident, I have tried harder to keep my distance from Aimee. She very sweetly sent me a text from her personal phone afterwards, telling me that she would handle Nora. The next day, she very sweetly sent me another text informing me that she had handled it and that we don't have to worry about Nora telling Keaton anything. I didn't ask for clarification. I thanked her and then continued to keep my distance. It's now the end of the third week of Aimee's temporary stay at the Snap-Legal offices, and the only thing this distance has created is even more desire to be near her. All the time.

As a founding CEO, I answer questions all day long, prioritize and try to find solutions. But the one thing that I can't seem to answer is: What's more important to me—the success of my company, Keaton's friendship, or a relationship with Aimee? And why can't I have all three of them now?

It's Friday night, and a few of us are going to have

to pull an all-nighter to get the new website pages up on schedule. I've given everyone on the team a ninety-minute break for dinner before we reconvene at the office, so I do what I always do when I'm questioning myself and I've finally had enough of drinking scotch at home while staring out a window. I've come to the restaurant to see my parents. My mother's face and soothing voice is minestrone soup for the soul, and my dad's tough love is whiskey for the heart.

When I was second-guessing my decision to make Keaton my CFO, listing all of the reasons no one else would give him that position, all they asked was if I trust him as a person. A lot of people would make a qualified Chief Financial Officer, but how many of them could I trust with my first baby? Even before I step inside, I know what it is I'm hoping to hear from them. Sometimes it just helps to hear someone else say it.

Locanda Graziella has remained an institution in Park Slope, in a saturated and ever-changing market. With a prime corner location on a pretty residential intersection and warm atmosphere, it's never without customers. It's a nice night, so most guests are seated outside on the wraparound patio. I find Maria, the middle-aged hostess who has worked here for two decades, standing at her post, covertly scrolling through Instagram on her phone. She was my de facto babysitter for years. She doesn't even look up when I approach her.

"What are you doing here alone on a Friday night? You're a good-looking guy. Go Tinder someone."

"That how you greet all your customers? I don't

know how my parents stay in business."

"I saw you crossing the street, all brooding-like. You know who else saw you? Three hot chicks who were crossing the street and you didn't even notice them."

"Why would I when I know the hottest chick in Brooklyn is waiting for me here?"

She finally gives me a hug. "Oh fuck you. You working out more or something? You look healthier."

"I quit smoking."

"Shut up."

"I did."

"How?"

"Iron will."

"Why?"

"You kidding?"

"Ohhhh." She gives me her knowing look. "A girl." She smacks my chest with the back of her hand. "No wonder you're so broody. Chase McKay. Finally got caught."

"I'll just seat myself, thanks."

I head for the back-corner table, nodding at the few other patrons inside.

Maria follows me. "You want me to get your mom? I think your dad's out back on the phone."

"Yeah, thanks. I'll just be here, brooding."

I sit down and pull out my personal phone, open up Aimee's text messages to re-read them like some teenage girl. She is so fucking sweet and funny, it hurts. I didn't ask her to stay at the office tonight, although it wouldn't have been outside her duties as project manager at all. I just felt it would be too tempting, having her around at night. Even with five other people there.

My mom comes out from the kitchen, wiping her hands on her white apron. She's a foot shorter than me but she fills every room she's in with her big, glowing personality. I get up to hug her, letting her warmth permeate me.

"Hey, Ma."

"*Il mio bel ragazzo,*" she coos. My beautiful boy. We sit down and she reaches across the bistro table to push my hair out of my face. "Good," she says, approving. "Good length. You gonna stay and eat?"

"Yeah, I've got an hour or so."

"Jimmy! Jimmy!" My mom calls the waiter over.

"Hey Chase! Good to see you, man!"

"New ink?" I ask, eyeing his forearms.

"You like? Your ma doesn't."

My mother waves her hand in her face. "Too much! Too much! Both of you."

"I like it."

"Put in his usual order, please Jimmy."

"You got it."

As soon as Jimmy's gone, my mom's staring at me. "Whatsa matter, uh?" Her voice is low and deep, and all of a sudden, so Italian. "You look tired. You working too hard again?" And then she stares at me harder and clutches at her chest. "*Dio mio!* No! Chase? You're in love!"

How is it these two women can tell in three seconds, but my best friend and the woman I'm falling for don't have a clue?

"Shhh. Ma."

"Don't you shush me! My only son is in love again, finally, with something other than work! I should be singing from the roof! Who is she? Where is she? Why you're not telling me anything?!"

"If you'd just give me a chance …"

She mimes buttoning up her mouth and gestures for me to proceed.

"Her name is Aimee. You'd like her. She's sweet, but she's got the fire in her too … I met her over a month ago. At Bitters. But then Keaton showed up, and I could tell he really liked her, so I decided to back off."

"What's this backing off? What's that mean?"

"I mean I left, so he could keep talking to her."

"She liked Keaton better than you?" My mother is appalled by this notion.

"Turns out she didn't, but you know how he is when it comes to girls."

"I never understand why you treat him like he's a spoiled little boy. If he's your friend, he's you're friend. Simple."

"I thought I was making it easier for everyone. Turns out it made things more complicated. She didn't want to go out with him and then I ran into her again a month later and we had one beautiful night together."

"Ohhh good! So what's the problem?"

"The problem is, it turns out she was hired to do some consulting work for us at the office."

"Uh huh …" Her voice goes even deeper, and I can tell she's still waiting to hear what the problem is.

"Hey! Chase, my boy! Why didn't you tell me he

was here?" My dad's booming voice competes with the Sinatra from the house speakers.

"He just got here!"

I get up to give my dad a quick hug.

"Where's your drink?"

"Don't have one yet."

My dad grabs a bottle of Redbreast and a tumbler from the bar. "Why's he so tired? Girl trouble?"

"Hmm. Making trouble for himself, this one."

"What else is new?" My dad slams the bottle and glass on the table in front of me, sits down in the chair near my mom. "She married?"

"No."

"Boyfriend?"

"No."

"Girlfriend?"

"No."

"Lives somewhere else?"

"No."

"So? What's the trouble?"

"His head is what's the trouble! Too much thinking, not enough living."

"I heard that!" Keaton's voice is unexpected, but I'm hardly surprised. He's on a roll when it comes to showing up at the wrong time lately. But he's so happy to see us, I can hardly resent him.

"What're you doing here?"

"I have to meet Quinn for a drink in an hour, I thought I'd grab a bite."

"Who's this lucky girl, Quinn? It's a girl, yes?"

Keaton laughs. "It's a girl, yes. A very pretty girl."

"A socialite," I add.

"A fancy girl!"

"Sounds like trouble to me," my dad says, as he gets up to take a call on his cell phone. "Chase here's got girl troubles."

"Oh yeah? I didn't realize there was a girl to trouble you."

"He doesn't know what he's talking about. Let's get you a drink."

"The usual for you boys, yes?" My mother gets up and gives Keaton a hug and a kiss.

"It's good to see you, Graziella."

She pats him on the arm. "You are always welcome here, *tesoro*." She blows me a kiss, and Keaton takes her vacated seat.

He calls out to Jimmy, who's behind the bar, asking for a gin and tonic.

"Look at you, out of the office and I didn't even drag you here."

"I'm heading back in an hour."

"Why?"

I laugh. "The new web pages go up tomorrow. We're fine-tuning."

"Oh yeah. You need me there?"

I laugh. *As if.* "We're good, thanks."

"Aimee gonna be there?"

I shake my head. "We can reach her if we need her."

He nods. "Yeah. Lucky you."

I manage to swiftly change the subject and spend the next half hour shooting the shit with him and remembering why Keaton is my best friend. It's good, even though it makes me feel guiltier and more hesitant about wanting to be with Aimee. I try not to ask about Quinn too much, so it doesn't seem like I'm pushing him to be with her. He sounds pretty whipped, and not as happy as he could be. But that's what Keaton's like when he's dating. Once he's got the girl, he gets anxious and feels trapped. The pursuit is definitely his favorite part. To be honest, I usually like him more when he's in pursuit of someone or something. At least he's working. As long as he doesn't try to pursue Aimee again, we're all good.

He gets a text from Quinn, telling him that she's on her way to the lounge. Early. He wipes his mouth with the napkin and reaches for his wallet. "The lady beckons," he says.

"You don't have to pay."

He leaves a hundred-dollar bill, as always. "Say goodbye to your parents for me."

"You guys in town this weekend?"

He nods. "See you Monday. Aimee's last week, right?"

"I guess so, yeah."

He furrows his brow. "We never got a chance to talk about your girl troubles."

"It's not a thing."

"That's right. Chase McKay never has any trouble with the girls."

If you only knew.

Almost as soon as Keaton is gone, my parents come back out to join me. I hold up the hundred-dollar bill for my mom. "He insisted. He says goodbye."

My mom shakes her head. "You keep it."

"We'll take it." My dad puts it in his pocket. "Put it towards your organic white truffle olive oil." He turns to me. "Your ma filled me in. What are you? Nuts?"

"Maybe."

"Going after the woman you love doesn't make you a bad friend to Keaton or a bad leader." He thumps his chest. "It makes you a man. You think I stopped to worry about the other guys who wanted your mother? Half the men in Brooklyn wanted to marry her."

My mother shrugs. "There weren't as many men in Brooklyn back then."

"Stop worrying so much, boy. If Keaton can't deal with it, you deal with that later. You can deal with it. He's entitled, but he's good."

"He's got a girlfriend!" My mom makes a very Italian gesture with her hands.

"For now."

My dad pats me on the back. "Don't be such a pussy, will ya? If it comes down to it, you guys just need to kick each other in the balls and be done with it." He goes over to another table, to check on the customers.

I smile at my mom, who's shaking her head.

"You and Keaton. You're like brothers with the— *rivalità tra fratelli.*"

"Sibling rivalry."

"Yeah! Both different, both want to be more the same, but better. But you're afraid to really act like brothers."

"You think we should kick each other in the balls too?"

She holds her hands up in front of her chest. "I'm not saying this!"

"Trust me, I'd love to. Gotta get back to the office."

"Friday night?"

"We've got a deadline." I start to bus the dishes.

"Why you always gotta work so hard, huh? Leave it! Leave it!" When I was a kid, she was always yelling at me to bus the tables, now she yells at me to leave it.

"It's in the blood. Why did you guys always work so hard?"

"Oh, *vita mia*. For you! For each other! You listen. I know how much you care about this girl because of how much you are thinking and planning and worrying —just like with your business idea. You were lucky nobody did your business idea before you did. But in New York City? A special girl gets done by another man like *that!*" She snaps her fingers.

"Oi! Get back in the kitchen, woman!" my dad yells out to her.

My mom flips him off, Italian-style. It's all part of the show and the customers love it.

She grabs my face with one hand and squeezes. "Time for you to get your own pain in the ass to come home to."

I kiss her on both cheeks, and she's back in the kitchen.

Stepping out into the night, I look up and silently curse the sky for reminding me of Aimee's dark blue eyes. Then, as always, I casually scan the streets and sidewalks for her, wondering where she is and why I'm not calling her.

CHAPTER 17
AIMEE

"Put your damn phone away."

"They're working on the website. I'm on call."

"He's not going to call you."

"I can't believe he hasn't called me. He hasn't even asked me about Nora."

Roxy signals to the waitress to bring us two more margaritas and more chips for our artichoke dip. Every now and then, Roxy gets a hankering for TGI Fridays, and I am more than happy to oblige when she begs me to join her, because no one else in Brooklyn will. Sometimes a girl just wants a couple of margaritas and about seven appetizers. Tonight, a girl needs about seven margaritas and half of the menu.

"Did Nora like the free shit I got her?"

"Yes. Thank you." I got Roxy to bring home free shit from the online store she works for. I did this after telling Nora, in confidence, that I had met Chase before meeting Keaton and that Chase had backed off when he saw that Keaton liked me. Because Nora didn't give a rat's bum about people's feelings, but she did need a new wardrobe. "And she wore the shoes for her date tonight."

"You think that'll work out?"

"God, I hope so." I had noticed Nora trying to flirt with a guy who works in the office across the hall from SnapLegal when we were all at the coffee shop downstairs, so I invited him to sit with us. I started asking them both what they were into, for fun, and kept asking until they finally mentioned the same thing. So tonight, Nora and the across-the-hall guy are going to some weird sexy circus party thing, with aerialists and energy clearing sessions in Bushwick. Kids today! I hope she gets the energy banged clear out of her, so she doesn't give a shit about other people's business anymore. She had every intention of telling Keaton what she'd heard in the break room, just because she was bored and wanted to stir up trouble. But I handled it. I managed that project and worked it like a pimp. And all I got from Chase was a very professional and courteous thank you.

"Ladies, these are from the gentlemen at table nineteen. With the wings platter." Our waitress wearily places two more strawberry margaritas in front of us. "And here are your extra chips."

Roxy and I cautiously look over at the buffalo wing gentlemen at table nineteen, and they are everything we expect them to be. I raise my glass and mouth "thank you" to them, but Roxy kicks my shin and ignores them.

"Ow!"

"Do not encourage them."

"It's rude not to thank people." I reach for my phone.

"Do not take a picture and text it to Chase to let him know that other men are buying you drinks."

"I wasn't going to!"

I am totally going to. I hate that she knows me so well. I take a picture of the margaritas and text it to Chase's personal phone.

ME: *Just checking in! I'll be here at TGI Friday's if you need me. Some very friendly gentlemen just sent us over these drinks, but I want you to know that I am still very lucid and capable of advising your team remotely if necessary. Also fully able to fend for myself in case of zombie apocalypse, so no need to worry.*

And—send!

I feel really good about that text. And super tipsy.

I pretend to be completely focused on whatever it is that Roxy is talking about for the next three minutes while I wait for Chase to respond to my adorable text, but he doesn't. However, my hands are trembling when I pick up my work phone, to read the Slack message he has sent me on one of the group channels.

CHASE: *@Aimee your presence is kindly requested here at the office, if you are available. Please come ASAP and be prepared to pull an all-nighter with the team. Thx.*

"An all-nighter!" I squeal.

"Do not leave me with the buffalo wing guys."

"Oh, honey, I would never. Hurry up and finish. I have to go pull an all-nighter. With the team. For work."

"Don't write him back yet."

"I'm not."

I totally am.

AIMEE: *Please expect my presence shortly. Should I bring snacks?*

Oh God, do I want to be his naughty little late-night snack.

CHASE: *Yep.*

———

By the time Roxy and I have finished wolfing down our drinks and appetizers, I am teetering on the edge of tipsy and about to stumble into drunkity drunkville.

Roxy walks me to the office building, helping me carry the takeout Philly cheesesteak egg rolls and loaded chicken nachos, and then she takes a cab home. I am so glad I don't have to go to the party that I had agreed to go to with her tonight. I can't imagine a better Friday night than working with Chase and the website team. I can't believe I was so worked up about having to be around Chase for the past three weeks. All I needed was a little tequila, triple sec, agave syrup and pureed strawberries. Or a lot of it.

I walk in a totally straight line to the building entrance and eventually manage to open the door. I nod at the gentleman who is also waiting for the elevator. I am standing so straight and still that there is no way he can tell I just consumed three margaritas. When he holds the elevator door open and allows me to enter first, I curtsy and laugh, because I'm hilarious—not because I'm drunk.

"What floor?" he asks.

"Yes, thank you," I say. Eventually, I remember which floor SnapLegal is on.

When I get off on the floor that I thought SnapLegal was on, I pretend to know where I'm going, until the elevator doors close again. Instead of waiting for the next elevator, I take the stairs. As soon as I'm in the stairwell, I hear the voice.

The voice that always sounds like sexy phone voice, even when he's not on the phone.

The voice that flooded my panties when he sang happy birthday while playing the keyboard with those perfect fingers.

The voice that—come to think of it—I have never actually heard on the phone pressed up to my ear unless we're on a conference call.

But he's talking to someone on the phone, one floor up. It echoes around the stairwell and around my belly.

"Naw, we got it covered," he says. "I'll be here all night; I was just letting you know what's up. Go back to your future in-laws." He laughs. "Well, I can't help you there. Bye."

He was probably talking to Greg Lee, and he was probably up on the roof deck.

I realize I've been tiptoeing up the steps like a creeper. When I hear his footsteps getting louder, I start stomping my heels. His footsteps slow down. We reach the landing at the same time.

He stops near the door to the hallway, sliding his phone into the back pocket of his jeans, and crosses his arms in front of his chest. He smirks as he observes me, standing here with two big TGI Fridays bags. When I try to stand still, I wobble, just a little.

"Are you drunk?" he asks.

"Yep."

I drop my satchel and the take-out bags, take three steps towards him, grab a fistful of his T-shirt and pull him to me.

When my lips touch his, I let out a sigh that fills the whole building.

I feel my entire body melting, my knees getting weak.

Chase maneuvers me against the door, pressing his pelvis against mine, his hands up in my hair.

Oh, those lips.

That facial hair.

That hard body.

His hands grip my waist as his tongue probes deeper into my mouth. We have an entire hungry breathless conversation with our lips and tongues, but he is saying so much more to me than he has said in weeks. I can taste the Irish whiskey and hunger and possessiveness. I am so deliciously and deliriously overwhelmed by this kiss that my arms just hang by my side. Now I know—I know that he's missed this as much as I have. He has struggled with this as much as I have. Lowering his head to kiss my neck, he moans as his hands slide down to my ass and squeeze, hard.

"Oh God, Chase!" I don't say it very loud, but my words echo.

While those three little words are still reverberating up and down around the stairwell, he pulls away from me.

He curses under his breath and rests his hands on his hips, staring at the floor, shaking his head.

We both wipe our mouths and straighten up.

I nearly stumble as I reach down for my satchel, but I manage to compose myself.

"I'm not going to apologize for that," I say, tossing my hair over one shoulder.

"I'm not complaining."

"Good. I'll see you after I freshen up."

His head falls back. He rubs his face vigorously. "Uh huh."

When I turn on the light in the ladies' room, it is so bright, my eyes immediately squeeze shut. I have to lean against the wall to steady myself. If this isn't love, then I don't think I can handle the real thing. I feel dizzy, in the best possible way.

Or…possibly in the worst way ever.

Roxy always places an elastic hair band around my wrist when we drink tequila, because every time she makes me drink it, I throw up, even though I truly believe that I couldn't possibly ever throw up again. Every. Time.

I drop my satchel while tying my hair back and running for the toilet.

Absolutely everything that I had consumed tonight, with such passion and reckless abandon, is expelled from my body until I am praying for a swift death and vowing to do things differently from now on.

I am empty and humiliated and numb.

Yeah.

This feels like love.

CHAPTER 18
CHASE

That was by far the best thing that has ever happened to me in this building, no matter how much it hurt to stop.

A full minute after Aimee left the stairwell, I pick up the bags of takeout, and consider taking them downstairs to give them to the nearest homeless person I can find. But I bring them into the office and tell the gang that I ran into Aimee in the hall. The tech geeks are all so happy that she brought warm food. I'd told them to go out and have dinner earlier, but they just pounded energy drinks and scarfed down protein bars as usual.

There's music playing and I've been making coffee for everyone, so it's a pretty fun atmosphere when we work late to meet deadlines. I may demand excellence from my employees, but I insist that they enjoy their work. I just don't want anyone to enjoy their work quite as much as Aimee and I just did, when we're dealing with something as important as our website. Which is why I'm planning to keep my distance from Aimee tonight, while also keeping her away from idiots who buy her margaritas.

But when she walks in through the front door, it's clear to me that I won't have to worry about anything happening between us again this evening. She is walking very slowly and moving carefully, keeping her eyes on the ground. Whatever perfume she uses, she has applied twice as much as she usually does. When the guys thank her for the appetizers and ask if she wants any, she grimaces and backs away from the open takeout containers. I go to the break room to see if I can find her some ginger ale and a sleeve of saltine crackers.

She's a trooper. She manages to answer everyone's questions, keeping her head and body very still and barely opening her mouth to speak. She sends off more emails to our customer service team, to make sure they are ready for basic customer questions once the changes go live. All of this without complaining or mentioning anything about how she's feeling.

I go to my office to work on some reports for the board, and the next time I come out to check on everyone, Aimee is curled up on a sofa asleep. I carefully place my leather jacket over her. Even now, she is so beautiful, I ache for her. Those long dark eyelashes flutter. I can see her eyeballs moving behind her closed eyelids and wonder if she's dreaming of me.

At around 6 a.m., we're ready to go live with the new web pages, and I tell them to wait until Aimee's had a look at them first. I bend down by the sofa and softly say her name. She twitches before opening her eyes. As soon as she sees me, she hums and smiles. I want to kiss her so bad, but when she starts to reach out for me, I stand up straight and take a step back.

"We're about to go live, you want to have a look first?"

"Oh yeah. Thanks." When she realizes that my leather jacket is covering her, she looks so happy and I just want to kiss her again. She sits up slowly and arranges my jacket so it's hanging from her shoulders, rubbing her lips together as she looks around. I open up the bottle of water that's in my hand and give it to her. She smiles, gratefully, and I want to kiss her again. I always want to kiss her, and I'm starting to think that might not be such a big problem.

Once the new web pages are live, and we're officially offering subscription services to our customers, I call in a big delivery breakfast order. I catch Julia watching Aimee and me when we're chatting and eating, but she doesn't make a big deal. I'm not worried about Julia. I'll have to remember to ask Aimee about Nora, though, when we're alone together. Whenever that will be.

Midway through breakfast, Aimee excuses herself to answer her cell phone. She goes into the break room for privacy. I hear her say "mom" and "dad" and I can tell from the tone of her voice that her mom and dad are stressed about something. When she hasn't come out after five minutes, I poke my head into the break room and wait for her to acknowledge me. She looks so anxious, and I don't like it.

She waves me in.

"Mom just call the police! It's your property and he's breaking the law … Daddy, will you tell her? … Oh my God …Well then, I don't know what you want me to do about it. You asked me for my opinion and that's my opinion. Kick the fucker out onto the street where he belongs! … I don't care who his parents are—you were doing them a favor and now this guy is being a total asshole and costing you money."

I can't for the life of me figure out what this call is about.

"Mom. Mom! I'm at work, okay. I will call you again in an hour and we will try to figure out what your options are, but I can't promise you I'll change my mind about calling the cops … I love you. Bye." She hangs up and rubs her forehead. "Sorry. Is everything okay with the website?"

"Yeah. I'm checking on *you*. What's going on?"

"Ugh. It's so annoying. Trust me, you don't want to know."

"Trust me. I do."

"Okay, well my mom thought it would be fun to flip houses for extra income because she watches HGTV. And she has this friend who told her that her son is a carpenter who can help her do the renovations for a lot cheaper than what contractors were bidding. She said he'd finish the work a lot faster because it would be his only job. So my mom hired this guy, and it turns out he's kind of a mess and kind of a dick. Not only has he been doing crap work that she's going to have to hire someone to re-do, but he's been living on the premises and he refuses to leave. He's been convicted of two felonies before, and his parents swear he's been trying to go straight and stay sober. They're afraid that if my mom calls the cops or takes some kind of legal action that his life will be over. Meanwhile, each month that she can't sell the place, she's paying more on this mortgage. Money that she hadn't budgeted for. Anyway, my mom and dad are both college professors and they're just too nice, and they keep calling me for advice, but they don't want to take legal action because they don't want to upset the asshole's family. I called him and he hung up on me. I left him voice messages and I've sent him strongly-worded text messages. None of it matters to the guy."

My hands are balled up into fists. "Why didn't you tell me about any of this?"

She gives me a look. "You're kidding, right?"

I nod once. I get it. I deserve that. "If you've got plans for the rest of the day and tomorrow, you need to change them."

She blinks. "Why?"

"Because we're going to take care of this."

She blurts out some kind of laugh. "What? The house is in Ann Arbor. Ann Arbor, Michigan."

"I am aware of where Ann Arbor is located."

"Wait, so … you're saying you want to go with me to Ann Arbor? To deal with this asshole?"

"Yeah. I'll book us a flight out of Laguardia. Fly into Detroit, right? What's that, like a two-hour flight?"

"Yes." She looks so confused, but I am so clear on my mission.

"Let's go to our apartments to shower and change. A noon flight should be easy to make. Work for you?"

"Chase. Why would you do this when you've barely been speaking to me the past few weeks?"

"Because your family has a problem and I can fix it. Because I care about you. Because having boundaries and priorities and causes for concern doesn't mean that I don't have feelings or memories or desires or goals or needs. Because I want you to be happy. That okay with you?"

Her lower lip quivers. Her pretty deep blue eyes are moist. She nods her head, and I walk out to check out flights on my laptop.

I've got a buddy who's a badass lawyer in Detroit, but I've known assholes like this guy, assholes who won't listen to reason. They only respect one thing, and I cannot wait to be the guy who shoves that thing in his face.

CHAPTER 19
AIMEE

I can't believe I'm in Michigan with Chase McKay.

There are weekends where I don't even leave my apartment, but it's only Saturday afternoon and already I've gotten drunk on margaritas, made out with a guy that I'm crazy about, barfed, worked, slept, showered, and flown on a plane to my hometown. I am crushing it!

I wish we were here for a more pleasant reason, and I'm a little nervous about what it will be like when he comes face-to-face with the turd who's being a dick to my mother, but I am so grateful and turned-on that I sort of hope I get to see Chase give that asshole what he deserves.

My mom has described this man—Jason—as "tall and strong and not very polite." It's not like either of the felonies that he was convicted for were violent, but he still sounds like trouble. When I called to tell my mom that a male friend and I are coming to deal with this, she said, "Oh Aimee, you never told us you have a boyfriend! What's he like?!" As if she didn't have a squatter making her life hell right now. As if I could call Chase my boyfriend, or come even close to describing what he's like in words.

Chase spent most of the flight working on his laptop, while I slept and rehydrated. Once we land, he leans across the armrests and says, "C'mere," before kissing me. Just like that, I'm flying again. He finally asks me about how I handled the Nora situation. When I'm done explaining and tell him that Nora and the across-the-hall guy are actually dating now, he kisses me again, eyes sparkling.

"You're good," he says.

"At what?"

"At being a person."

That might be the nicest thing anyone has ever said to me.

Especially within twenty-four hours of me hurling.

We rent a car, and I insist on driving to my parents' house. We have to stop by there first, to pick up the key to the income property. Despite clearly being uncomfortable with a woman driving him, Chase is more relaxed and polite about it than most of the men I've driven around Michigan—including my dad.

"What are your parents like?" he asks.

"Kind. Nerdy. My mom's an English professor and my dad's a scientist. He mostly does research in molecular biology at the university. They were college sweethearts. Mary and Richard Gilpin."

"And you're an only child?"

"Yes. You?"

"Yes." He reaches over to rest his hand on my thigh. "You live in Ann Arbor your whole life?"

"Until I moved to New York. You haven't been before, have you?"

"No, but I drove down to Detroit with some friends for a concert once, in high school."

"Which one?"

"Chris Cornell at the Fillmore."

"Oh God. When he hung himself here, it was all anyone was talking about for a week. So sad."

"He had an incredible voice."

"Yeah …" I wait an appropriate and respectful amount of time before saying: "You know, when I first saw you, I thought you were the lead singer of a grunge band or something."

He laughs. "You wouldn't be the first. Maybe in my next life."

"I never would have guessed you're a CEO entrepreneur with a business and law degree, but it just makes you so … interesting … and *hawt.*"

He looks out the passenger window, silent, and for a moment I completely regret saying that. Did I insult him? It was meant to be a huge compliment.

He squeezes my thigh. "You want to know what I thought when I first saw you?"

"Oh God, I don't know. Do I? What?"

"I thought you were the most beautiful woman I'd ever seen, and I thought to myself: 'Wow. So this is what love at first sight feels like.'"

I slam on the brakes.

Fortunately, we're on a side street and no one is behind us.

"Jesus."

He looks over at me. "You okay?"

I shake my head. "Wow, when you talk, you really *say* stuff, don't you?"

"Sorry if I don't talk enough."

"I am not complaining."

"You should probably drive, though."

"Right." I step on the gas, just as another car turns onto the street. "We're almost at my parents' house. Last chance to get out and run back to the airport."

"I'm looking forward to meeting the people who made you," he says, smiling.

I check the rearview mirror, disappointed that there's a car behind me, because I desperately want to stop and make out with Chase again before seeing my mom and dad.

My parents still live in the house I grew up in, in the Old West Side. It's a lovely treelined street. All historic houses with front porches and polite, friendly neighbors.

It's not until I'm knocking on the front door that it occurs to me—my parents might be a little surprised by the kind of guy Chase is, or the way he looks, anyway. I immediately feel guilty for even having the thought, and protective of him. I take his hand and squeeze it.

We can hear my mom yelling for my dad, from just behind the door. She's jumping up and down and reaching out to hug me even before she's completely opened the door.

"My baby! This is such a wonderful surprise!"

"Hi Mom."

"We both woke up feeling so crappy and now you're here and we're so happy. Oh look at that! I just rhymed!"

"My mom's a regular Dr. Seuss. Mom, this is my friend from New York, Chase McKay."

Chase steps out from behind me. "Hello."

"Ooohh!" My mother clutches her chest and giggles and blushes. "Oh my! Hellooo."

Oh God.

"Well, aren't you nice-looking."

Oh no.

"It's very nice to meet you, Professor Gilpin." Chase shakes hands with my mother. He's wearing his jacket, so his tattoos aren't visible, but his genius is. Calling my mother "Professor Gilpin" even off-campus is the way to her heart. So is looking like the lead singer of a grunge band, apparently.

"Oh please, call me Mary." She looks at me. "He has such beautiful hair! So nice-looking! *And* you're a lawyer?!"

Chase is trying so hard not to laugh.

"He's the CEO of a legal tech—you know what—we'll talk about this later."

I widen my eyes at her. *Calm down.*

"Who's nice-looking?!"

"Richard! Aimee's here, and she's brought her friend Chase!"

"They're here already?!" My dad shuffles to the door. I don't think I've ever seen my dad in a hurry in his life. "Aww, there's my girl."

"Come in! Come inside!" My mom waves us in.

"Actually, we just came to get the key from you and then we're going to take care of, you know. *The thing.* We'll see you afterwards."

"Gimme a hug." My dad comes onto the porch to hug me. I can feel it when he looks over at Chase. "Well, now." He lets go of me. "I see you brought us a beef-cake New York rock star to kick some butt."

"Dad!" I turn to Chase. "I'm horrified."

"It's good to meet you, Professor Gilpin. I'm happy to kick some butt for a good cause, but I'm hardly a rock star."

"Well, I've been wanting to kick that guy's butt, but Mary here won't let me."

"Oh. Pssh!" My mom hands me the key for the house. "I feel so badly about this. I don't want you to get hurt, Chase. I mean, I don't think Jason has a gun or anything, he's just a bit of a dick, as Aimee would say. Aimee—you stay in the car."

"Aimee will definitely be staying away from the house when Jason is there, and I don't intend to use physical force unless it's necessary. Otherwise my business and law degrees were a waste of time. But I have a feeling it might be necessary with that guy."

I can literally see the wheels turning in my mom's head and cartoon hearts flying around as she's picturing what our kids will look like.

"True dat," my dad says.

"Dad. Don't say 'true dat.' Ever."

"Sorry, honey. *Word.*"

"We have to go."

"Mary, you should call a locksmith to go to the house and meet us there as soon as possible. We'll let you know when it's safe to come join us, okay?"

My mother clasps her hands together in front of her chest and nods.

"Please don't worry. It'll be fine." Chase takes my hand and leads me down the porch steps.

"You call us if you need anything!"

I turn back to my dad. "Will do!"

My mom mouths to me: "He's so handsome!"

"I know!" I mouth back.

"I'm going to grow my hair long!" my dad stage whispers, loud enough for Chase to hear.

Chase has me pull over to park across the street and half a block down from the house in question. There's a shiny truck parked in the driveway, so it looks like Jason is there now.

"Aww, man! I wanna watch!"

"You can watch from here. I don't want you in the street in case this guy drives off really fast. And I don't want him to see a car pull up in the driveway. Where's your phone?"

I pull it out of my pocket.

"I'm texting you the contact info for my buddy Lars. He's an attorney here in Detroit. If shit goes down, you call him and tell him you're my girlfriend. He knows we're here. Hang tight."

I grab his arm. "Say that again."

He laughs, as he looks at his phone. "I told him you're my girlfriend. You know. Made it easier to ask him for a favor."

I smash my lips against his cheek. "I love you!" I blurt out. And then I cover my mouth, because *shit what did I just say?*

"I love you too," Chase says, like we've been saying it to each other forever.

In some way, I guess we have.

"Oh my God, please be careful."

"It'll be fine. Trust me. But leave the engine running, just in case."

He gets out of the car, removes his jacket and leaves it in the passenger seat. I guess he figures he looks more badass when his ink is showing and he is absolutely right. He strides toward the house, looking like a beefcake rock star who's about to kick some butt. I watch until he has reached the front door and uses the key to go inside. He leaves the front door open.

"Oh my God oh my God oh my God," I mutter to myself.

My hands are trembling as I text my parents to let them know that we are here.

I text Roxy, to let her know that we just said "I love you" to each other.

Roxy immediately replies with dancing lady, raising hands, heart and party popper emojis.

My mom replies with heart, bride and groom and

baby emojis. I really don't know if she has her priorities straight right now. But it still makes me happy.

Whatever this is between Chase McKay and me, no matter how frustrating it has been for me to get to this point—it works for me. In the way that breakfast for dinner works for me. I am so ready to eat a big stack of pancakes with this man tonight.

I don't even know how long I've been sitting here daydreaming with a dumb smile on my face, but all of a sudden, I see a man speed-walking out the door of the house my mother owns. He's carrying a toolbox and an overflowing duffel bag, and he is quickly followed by Chase, who is holding a bunch of power tools and looks enraged. I roll down the passenger window a crack so I can hear them.

The man tosses his stuff into the back of his truck and gets into the driver's seat, slamming the door shut. Chase dumps the power tools in the back of the truck and points at him: "The rest of your shit will be returned to your parents—who care about you even though you're a fucking asshole!" He goes around to the driver's side and bangs on the window. "If I hear you so much as drove past this house or did *anything* in *any way* to damage this property or upset the Gilpins again, I will *hunt you down and beat your ass* and you will be prosecuted to the fullest extent of the law. D*o. You. Understand?!*" He pounds on the roof of the truck. "Get out of here!"

The guy flips him off as he backs out of the drive-way, tires squealing. Chase flips him the bird right back, all the way down to the end of the driveway, for as long as it takes the guy to drive down the block. My heart is racing.

I wait until the truck has turned onto a cross street before slowly driving up to the driveway. Chase is waiting in the doorway for me. He is trying to catch his breath, but he nods and waves for me to join him. I look around to see if any neighbors are watching. If they are, they're doing it from inside their homes. I run inside the house to join him, throwing my arms around him.

"That was amazing!"

"That guy really was a dick, but he was also a dumbass."

"Did you have to fight him? Are you okay?!"

"I just went after him so fast and shoved him around, he didn't really have time to react. He was definitely stoned. This place reeks of pot."

I kiss him all over his face. "I can't believe you did this for my mom. Thank you thank you thank you."

"You should call them and tell them to come over so they can be here when the locksmith gets here. Let's start tidying up and airing this place out. He really did a shit job with the remodel." He is so angry; you'd think it was *his* mom's problem.

I love him.

I love everything about Chase McKay.

It stinks in here and there's so much to do, but I love him. I really love him.

Ten minutes later, my parents show up at the same time as the locksmith. Chase tries to clean up as much of the mess that Jason has left as possible, but my mom and dad insist that he stop so they can take us to dinner. Chase and I exchange a furtive look that tells me everything I need to know.

"We really have to get back to New York, you guys. We just launched this new thing for his business and it's important that we're around in case anything goes wrong. Chase just really wanted to take care of this as soon as possible."

"Oh, Chase." My mother hugs him. "How can we ever thank you?"

"This hug is enough," he answers. Then he pulls a piece of paper out of his pocket and hands it to her. "These are the names and numbers of my friend—the lawyer in Detroit—and a good contractor that my friend has used. He said he's affordable and trustworthy. If Jason or this contractor give you any trouble, you call my friend. He will help you."

My father has never approved of any boy or man that I've brought home to meet him in the past, but I can tell by the way he shakes Chase's hand that he not only approves of him, but he has a bit of a man crush.

"Well done, young man."

"Have a good night, sir."

When we're in the rental car, I turn on the engine and rub my lips together.

"You don't actually want to get back to New York right away, right?"

"No. I don't."

"Do you, um … Do you want to get some dinner or see some live music?"

"I want to go to the nearest hotel and get you naked immediately."

"Thank God."

For the second time today, tires squeal as a vehicle is backing out of that driveway.

CHAPTER 20
CHASE

By the time the heavy hotel room door is half-closed, I've got Aimee half-naked and backed up against a wall. She somehow manages to pull my shirt off while I'm removing her bra. Pressing myself against her, skin-to-skin, I don't even care about teasing or pacing or technique. I need to touch this woman and be inside of her more than I need to breathe. *Not* doing this has been slowly killing me, when all I want to do is live for her.

"I am so in love with you." The words come without me even realizing I'm saying them out loud.

She makes a sound that may or may not be a word. Something like *"nuh!"* but I know what she means. I know what she means to me and that's all that matters now.

I kiss her so hard, squeeze her hips even harder. I'd worry about bruising her, but she's coming at me with just as much force and urgency. An unspoken frantic plea for more. For everything. Every torturous aching second, all of the energy that we've spent holding back for weeks is compounded now in this resurgence.

I slide down to kiss her breasts, twirl my tongue around her hardened nipples, bite the swelled-up flesh and I make my way down, down, onto my knees and into my favorite place in the world. She calls out my name, over and over, a prayer and a tribute. Her hand fists my hair while my tongue slips in and out. Her trembling thighs want to press together, I know, because there's so much pressure in her clit.

I feel the pressure too, I'm about to explode, there's no way around it.

I pull her pants down to the floor so she can step out of them, dropping my pants to my ankles while standing back up.

"Get inside me," she whispers, but it's so loud to me I think all of Detroit must be able to hear her too.

I do. I get inside her, crying out like I'm in pain, and it feels so damn good. She curls one leg around the back of mine as I thrust up and into her, again and again, just this. This is everything I want, right here. Just this woman, all of her, all the time.

I slow down enough so that I can look at her. She opens her eyes, and in this moment that I'm staring into that deep blue from this close distance, I know exactly what our life together will be like from now on. I know what I'd risk losing just to keep her, and it doesn't even scare me. Because I know what I'm capable of building and rebuilding as long as I'm doing it for her. I'd do anything for her. I will.

———

Everything on this bed is sweaty and tangled up in each other. We're a jumbled mess of arms and legs and hair and sheets and pillows and empty room service plates, but everything feels like it's exactly the way it should be. My fingers find hers and interlace with them.

"I'm going to tell Keaton when we get back. Tomorrow afternoon, if possible, so he'll have time to cool off before work on Monday. I'm not going to hide this—us—anymore."

She takes a deep breath. "Are you sure?"

"I don't know if you've noticed, but I've been thinking about this a lot. I'm very sure."

"Do you want me to be there when you tell him?"

"No. But thank you for offering."

"I just don't want him to be mad at you."

"He can be mad. He'll get over it. Eventually."

"I just … it's not really about me, though? Right? I mean, Keaton barely knows me."

If this were any other woman, I'd tread lightly around this *do these pants make me look fat?* type of question. Since it's Aimee, I know she's really asking because she wants to understand. "It's a lot of things from over the years. I don't regret working with my best friend like this, but it does make things more complicated. Keaton may have his head up his ass a lot of the time, but he's an extremely loyal and generous person once he's decided someone really matters to him. As soon as he gets the idea in his head that someone isn't as loyal as they should be to him, he can

… be an unpredictable asshole. But like I said. He gets over it. Eventually."

"Okay. I hope so. I hope our last week of working together won't be tense and weird."

"Unlike our first few weeks of working together, you mean?"

"True," she says. "I guess we better make sure there's absolutely no chance of us feeling tense, then …"

I sit up and swipe my index finger across the remaining butter and maple syrup on a plate. She wanted breakfast for dinner, and we got it. I hold that finger over her mouth. She licks it, sucks on it, pulls me down to her so she can do the same to the rest of me.

"Chase McKay, you're so much, but I don't think I can ever get enough of you," she sighs.

"Good. I'm all yours and I don't plan on ever leaving you."

AFTER TODAY

CHAPTER 21
CHASE

get to Bitters about twenty minutes before five, which is when I asked Keaton to meet me here for a drink. I use the time to chat with Denny, get settled into a booth, respond to customers on Twitter, reminisce about the two times I've been here with Aimee, and get a head start on the whiskey. I might always feel like I'm making up for lost time with Aimee Gilpin, but after today, no one will be in the dark about how I feel about her. No matter how Keaton takes the news I'm about to give him.

Keaton shows up at exactly five o'clock, which is unlike him. He salutes me as he heads to the bar to order scotch. When Keaton orders scotch, it means he's either feeling shitty about his parents or his girlfriend. Or both. I watch him as he scans the room, his gaze resting on a pair of ladies at the end of the bar. Yeah. He is not happy with his sex life. That's unfortunate, but it doesn't change anything.

He exhales slowly as he sprawls out opposite me. "A booth tonight? We gonna make out?"

"Buy a guy a drink first."

"You want another?"

"Naw, not yet. How you doin'?"

"I don't even want to talk about it. So the new website's up. Everything's working. No customers have revolted yet. Right?"

"So far so good."

"What's on the agenda for the board meeting tomorrow?"

"The main thing I'm concerned with, besides updating on the subscriptions, is voting on our next hire."

"Right. Your underdog boy for the sales team."

"Danny's got the experience, he just doesn't have an Ivy League degree."

"But the other guy's got both."

"The other guy's got a lot less experience and I think Danny's a better fit for our culture. He's local."

"But we aren't going to be local forever."

"And when we go global we'll hire appropriately."

"I'm just busting your chops, kid. I like the guy, I'll back him. I don't know about the other guys on the board, though."

"That's why I need your vote on this."

"If it's that important to you. I got you."

"Good."

He squints at me. "You look like you've been on vacation or something."

I can't help smiling. "I did just get back from Detroit."

"Why would anyone willingly go to Detroit?"

"I went to Ann Arbor with Aimee."

I wait for a look of comprehension to register on his face.

"*Aimee* Aimee?"

"Aimee Gilpin. She ended up pulling an all-nighter with us Friday, and I found out her mom had this situation that needed fixing. So I went with her to take care of it. And we stayed the night."

Keaton hosted a weekly poker game when we were at Wharton. When they were at the apartment I was usually either studying at the library or out with some girl, because the last thing I wanted was to be around a bunch of cigar-smoking rich assholes. But I did watch my buddy play a few times, and he has a very impressive poker face. I'm looking at that poker face now, but I'm ready to show my hand anyway.

"We're together now. I fell for her the same night you did, only I did it about half an hour before you walked in. I backed off because it seemed like the right thing to do, and when you told me she finally shot you down a month later, I came here to give Denny my phone so I wouldn't call her. I wasn't planning to see her again, but she showed up here. Turns out she came to find me to talk about the job she'd just been hired for, but she didn't end up telling me that night."

His jaw is clenched tight, and he's getting that look in his eyes, but I keep going.

"We decided to have one amazing night together, to

get it out of our systems. I was going to tell you about it, but then she walked into our office and everything changed."

"You really didn't know about her job?"

"I just said. She never got around to telling me, until she was standing there in our office, telling both of us."

"So—what—you guys have been fucking behind my back for three weeks?"

"No. We've been *not* fucking for three weeks, but everything changed again this weekend. And it's a lot more than fucking. I love her. I'm not gonna hide it anymore. I want you to be okay with it, but we're together. *That's* not going to change."

He taps his fingers on the tabletop. "So you felt sorry for me?" He sneers. "You think she's so great I'd never get over losing her to you?"

"Watch it."

He shrugs. "I'm okay with you being with her. Good for fucking you, you deserve it. If you guys have been thinking I'm pining over her like some lovesick fool, you're sadly mistaken."

"Good to know."

"It is good to know things, isn't it? I would have liked to know. If you didn't trust me enough to tell me about this, that tells me a lot."

I shake my head, ever so slightly.

"If you decided to fuck her before discussing it with me first, that tells me even more."

"You were in the Hamptons with Quinn."

"Hoes before bros, right?"

"She gave me her number before you got here."

"Course she did. The ladies always go for the Irish-Italian Stallion. No wonder you had that genius idea to have her not cc me on anything. So I could stay focused on Quinn."

"It wouldn't have made a difference to Aimee."

"If you say so."

"She offered to come talk to you tonight too."

"Well that would have been a treat. Kind of the opposite of the time you and Whitney were both trying to convince me that you *hadn't* been fucking each other behind my back."

"Whitney and I never fucked." *Words I never thought I'd have to say out loud to him again.*

"Course not. It's all about transparency, right? You've always said if we're going to work together we have to be transparent and work shit out so the other investors don't get nervous."

"And that's what we're doing. You believe what you need to believe, Keaton. I know what you mean to me, which is why I tried to stay away from her. But this is real and it's happening and I hope you can feel as good about it as I would for you, if you were this happy."

His face twitches. My best friend's in there somewhere, he's just hiding under a few layers of pissy entitled asshole for now. He juts out his chin. "It's all good, man," he says.

I hold my hand out across the table. "No hard feelings? This is what it is, let's not let it affect anything else, alright?"

He shakes on it. "Lemme get you that drink so we can make out now—oh wait, you're taken."

I laugh. "So are *you*, right?"

"Sure." He signals to the waitress to bring us two more drinks. "She's met your parents?"

"Not yet, but I met hers, yesterday. In Ann Arbor."

"Nice. Look at us. Greg's getting married, we're both 'taken.' Fucking crushing this adulting thing."

We have a five-minute bullshit conversation about nothing much and then he's gone.

I'm not even worried about the shit he may or may not pull, because in fifteen minutes I'll be at Aimee's apartment and in her arms and I'll stay there until I wake her up in the morning.

CHAPTER 22
AIMEE

've been at my Hoffman & Company office for an hour so far this morning, meeting with future and potential clients, and I already miss the gang at SnapLegal. By "gang" I mostly mean Chase's penis, but the whole crew over there is great. Even Keaton and Nora. Even though I'll still be in touch with most of them on Slack for a while, I will be coming down off of quite a high when this week is over.

Or, maybe a new high will begin.

Chase was fairly tight-lipped, but somewhat optimistic after talking to Keaton yesterday evening. Having him in my apartment just felt so right. He and Roxy get along great, and we all just hung out for a couple of hours before Chase and I retired to my bedroom. The whole weekend was like some kind of amazing alcohol poisoning-induced fever dream.

I snap out of my daydream when Elaine Hoffman clears her throat. I have no idea how long she's been standing in my office, and I have no idea how long

I've been sitting here with a big stupid smile on my face.

"Am I interrupting?" she asks, while taking a seat at the chair in front of my desk.

"Not at all. Hi! What do you need? I just sent a follow-up email to—"

"I just wanted to check in with you about SnapLegal." She pulls a small bag of roasted chick peas from one of her pockets and pops them into her mouth. She holds the bag out to me, halfheartedly offering me some.

"No thank you, I'm good. SnapLegal has been great. The transition has been relatively smooth, really. I'd say that by this weekend, with the launch of the new web pages, things have been going really great."

"No trouble with Keaton Bridges?"

"Not that I'm aware of." Now I'm wondering if she knows something I don't. "Why?"

She shakes her head and is about to say something but then she starts coughing—choking on a chickpea.

I am poised to get up and Heimlich her, but I don't want to perform abdominal thrusts on my new boss unless it's absolutely necessary. "Are you … Can I? …"

She holds her hand up to stop me. I just really don't want her to choke to death before telling me if there's anything I should know about SnapLegal. After coughing so loud and long that I think I can hear one of her lungs being dislodged, she abruptly stops coughing. Her face is completely red, but she says very clearly: "Chase McKay has been saying good things. He's very impressed with you."

"Really?" My voice is so high-pitched I sound like a cartoon squirrel. "How so?"

She touches her throat and starts coughing again, for the longest most awkward thirty seconds of my very impatient life.

I'm not sure which of us is going to die first.

She suddenly stops coughing when a tiny piece of dried chickpea skin shoots out of her mouth. "Oh. There we go!" she says, clearing her throat.

"Can I get you some water?"

"Nope. I'm good."

"So … Chase?"

"He said he'd be happy to recommend you to anyone who's on the fence about hiring us. He's very impressed with the work you do."

"Oh." I smile. I try not to smile. I try not to look like I'm trying not to smile. "That's nice. That's nice to know. He's great too. They're all great. That's a really, really great company. I'm so grateful for this job." I really hope she can't tell that I'm thinking about Chase's penis right now.

"Mmhmm. How long have you been banging him?"

Now I'm the one having a coughing fit. She is smirking at me. She could definitely tell that I was having penis thoughts.

"Oh come on," she says. "I don't give a crap who you bang, as long as you do good work. As a business consultant, I mean. He's yummy."

"Uh huh. We've … it's only been since this weekend really. It won't affect anything about the way we work together for the next week, I promise you."

"Hah! Sure it won't." She waves her hand dismissively. "Oh, but there's nothing quite so titillating as an office romance, is there? The board room hand jobs. The office floor sex. The bathroom quickies. That's how I met my husband, you know?"

"In a bathroom? I mean—you had an office romance?"

"Yes. His best friend worked with us, and he liked me too, so Joe—my husband—let his friend take a whack at me first."

I wrinkle my brow. Is she kidding me with this?

"Well, I slept with him. You know, just to get it out of the way."

"With the best friend?"

"I mean, I liked Joe more. But I just knew I'd have to go through his friend to get to him. And then, one thing leads to another and you're having a three-way."

"Sure."

"Things get weird."

"Yeah."

"And they had a bit of a falling out. But Joe and I got married, so … worth it."

"Well that's … sweet! And now Joe is writing a novel, you said?"

"No, Corey, my current husband is writing a novel. Joe is now Josephine. He lives in L.A. We still sext now and then. Corey's fine with it."

"Well, Elaine Hoffman, you have had quite a life."

She runs her fingers through her hair. "You only get one life, and it's gone just like that. So, you know. I think a little office nookie is quite in order. At any age, really." She gets up and tosses the rest of the roasted chickpeas into my wastebasket. "Well. Back to work."

"Thanks, Elaine!"

I'm not exactly sure what I'm thanking her for, but it's probably for giving me permission to have office nookie with Chase McKay.

———

It's after seven pm. Chase and I have plans for a late dinner. While he's still working in his office, I have been casually wandering about the offices, checking to see if anyone else is still around. After poking my head into the break room, supply room, ladies' room and knocking on the men's room door, I skip on over to place the underwear that I've just removed into my bag. I peer into the glass wall of Chase's office, above the part that's frosted, and see that he's just sitting there looking at his laptop.

I knock while entering, and shut the door behind me, locking it.

He looks over at me, grinning.

"Okay, hot stuff," I announce. "We're the only ones here. Take off your pants and get on the floor. This is not a drill." I start hiking up my skirt to the top of my thighs.

His eyes sparkle.

The voice from the speaker of his office phone says: "For fuck's sake, please wait until I've hung up before doing that."

I slap my hands over my mouth. *Oh God.*

Chase laughs. "We'll continue this discussion tomorrow, Matt."

"And I thought *our* offices were fun," Matt remarks.

Chase hangs up.

"Chase! I am so sorry! Please tell me that wasn't a client or an investor!"

"It was my dad."

My eyes bulge out of their sockets.

"I'm kidding." He gets up and slowly walks towards me, his focus entirely on my bare thighs. "That was my buddy, Matt McGovern. He's going to do some pro bono work for our clients."

I start to tug down on the hem of my skirt. "This was a terrible idea. I'm crazy. You're making me crazy."

He stops me from pulling down my skirt. "Whatcha got on under there?"

"Nothing. How could you tell?"

His fingers graze my soaking wet entrance. I tense up at the slightest touch from him. My clit is already throbbing.

Leaning in, he whispers into my ear. "Because you're very efficient and have excellent time management skills." His voice is so sexy, he could read my ninth-grade chemistry textbook out loud and have me on the brink of orgasm before he finished the table of contents.

He leads me over to the sofa that's situated in front of the frosted glass. I have his pants and boxers down around his ankles, and in about one second, push him down and straddle him. I hold my breath as I center and slowly lower myself down onto his rock-hard erection, holding the base of his shaft. Taking him in is an exquisite ache and satisfying release, all at once, every time. I shift around a tiny bit, squeeze and release. The hiss as he draws breath through clenched teeth is a signal to continue, the following groan is my cue to settle in and begin to move my hips.

He drags his fingernails down my back. It feels so good through my cotton shirt. What feels even better is having his hands up my shirt, squeezing my breasts and teasing my nipples while I frantically pick up the pace. I have to. I couldn't care less about making this a quickie in case someone sees us—I just can't seem to control myself once he starts touching me. I grab onto that man bun with both hands and I ride him like a mechanical bull. I squeeze my thighs together tight around him, keeping my upper body loose, I rock back and forth and sway as he bucks and slams up against me. I will hold onto this man and never ever let go, but I am already clenching and spasming around his cock. I know that neither of us have much longer before we're both disappearing into waves of pleasure.

My voice is nothing but desperate panting whispers, and I am so blissed out, I can't even form words anymore. My body is just screaming *yes, yes, yes!* Surely this feeling will never end.

He gives my ass a squeeze and then wraps his arms around my waist, forcing me down onto him hard when he comes. There is such vulnerability and strength in his stillness. I love to watch him like this. His baritone groan is a sexy ballad that vibrates all the way through me. We are both shuddering for such a long time even as we hang onto each other like limp rag dolls.

Chase's heart beats fast and hard against my own chest, and my ears are ringing loudly, but we both hear a door slam shut not far away.

I duck down further, and Chase kisses my forehead.

"Shhh. It's okay," he whispers.

It's not.

I've only been here for a few weeks, but I know that the only person who'd be slamming that door right now is Keaton.

CHAPTER 23
AIMEE

Keaton comes out of his office just as we're walking out of Chase's. I quickly grab my laptop, shove it into my bag and smooth down my hair again, making sure my clothes are where they should be. I think I'd feel less guilty and self-conscious if my parents had walked in on us. Not that he walked in on us. But he must have seen something.

"You don't think he watched us, do you?" I'd whispered to Chase, after we heard the door slam shut.

"No way," he'd snorted. "He probably just caught a glimpse and then stormed off to his office. At least he let us know he's here."

"I guess."

Chase holds his hand out to me. I take it, and we walk towards the front door. I try to keep my chin up and a polite smile on my face. This is the first time I'm seeing Keaton today. The first time I'm seeing him since Chase had a talk with him yesterday evening. It took a lot of willpower for me to walk past a stationary store this morning and *not* buy him a card—but what kind of card would I give him? *Thank you in advance for not being a dick about this! My condolences for not choosing you over your best friend! Have a great summer—please don't bad-mouth me to potential clients just because I didn't go out with you!*

"Well, well," Keaton says. He is sneering, his voice dripping with sarcasm. "If it isn't Brooklyn's most discreet and professional couple."

"Nice to see you back at the office today," Chase says. "You forget something?"

"Yeah. I forgot to instill a sock-on-the-door policy," he says, in a way that makes it very difficult for me to tell if he's being funny or being a bitter asshole.

Chase squeezes my hand. "We're taking off. See you in the morning."

"Oh I'm taking off too." He follows us out to the elevators. God forbid he should make things less awkward and take the stairs. "Where are you two love-birds headed?"

"Taking her to the restaurant to meet my parents."

I stop in my tracks. This is news to me. I widen my eyes at him.

"You okay with that?" he asks me.

"Yeah, definitely." *I just wish I looked a little less freshly-fucked right now.*

"Aww, don't worry," Keaton says. "It's a cute little place. You'll like it."

"Yeah. It's a cute little place that Keaton can't seem to stay away from."

"What can I say, all those Michelin star restaurants

can get boring after a while. A guy needs a little variety. That's why I'm friends with Chase."

Keaton stands next to Chase, looking up at the illuminated floor numbers, grinning. "Sorry about this morning, buddy." He slaps Chase on the back. "Can't win 'em all."

I have no idea what he's referring to, but one look at Chase's clenched jaw and I know it's not nothing.

Keaton leans forward to give me a very obvious once-over. "You okay there, Aimee? You seem a little worn-out."

Wow. Okay. So he's a bitter and condescending asshole.

"Sorry you don't recognize what a woman looks like after having a *real* orgasm." Chase slaps him on the back. "Can't win 'em all."

Keaton fakes a loud laugh. "Brains *and* a sense of humor! And all this time I thought I was the lucky one, with the looks and the money."

My whole body tenses up. That cocky little shit. How dare he be condescending to my boyfriend. "For your information—"

Chase squeezes my hand again and cuts me off, just as the elevator doors open. "After you," he says to me. "I haven't told my parents we're coming yet," he says to me, completely ignoring Keaton. "So if you want to go somewhere else …"

"No, I would love to meet them!" I touch his face. "I can't wait to meet the people who made you."

"You'll like them," Chase says. "They're nice. Very supportive of me." He looks over at Keaton, who is shaking his head.

"Sounds like a cozy evening. I've gotta cross the bridge to meet Quinn. We're having dinner with a few Rockefellers tonight. Should be interesting."

"Sounds like fun. We'll save you a piece of tiramisu."

"Naw, I'm good. The desserts at Per Se are surprisingly filling."

I'm afraid they're about two seconds from whipping out their dicks and having a pissing contest right here in the elevator, but it is becoming very clear to me that Keaton is jealous of Chase and it has little to do with me. There's a lot of repressed *something* flowing beneath the surface of their relationship, like hot lava, and I do not want to be around when it finally erupts.

Mercifully, we reach the ground floor, and Keaton has pressed the button for the parking level. "You guys need a ride? Got the car. Gave my driver the day off because he was sick."

"We're gonna walk. See you tomorrow, man." Chase holds out his hand for one of those bro-shakes that men do.

"Say 'hi' to Graziella and Sean for me. Have a good night, Aimee." He is being so genuinely polite now. I honestly don't know how to read this guy, and I truly don't understand male friendships.

"You too," I say, more as a threat than I had meant for it to sound.

As soon as the elevator doors close, I ask: "What happened this morning, Chase? What was he talking about?"

He shrugs it off. "It's not a huge deal, but it really

pissed me off." He holds the lobby door open for me and waits until we're outside before continuing. "At the board meeting, we voted on our next hire for the sales team. I was backing this great guy who has the best resume, the best personality, the best track record. Except he didn't go to Harvard and he wasn't born the son of one of the investor's best friends. Keaton was going to vote with me, but he didn't."

"What a dick." I cover my mouth. "Sorry."

"Yeah, it was a dick move, but it didn't surprise me. It's not like the guy we are hiring is terrible, it's just not what I wanted. Sometimes you gotta step into the punch before it has time to develop, you know? Reduce the force of the blow. Better to take that hit now than further down the line when it's something more important."

"Is that a boxing metaphor?"

"Did you not learn that in business school?"

"I certainly didn't learn it in friendship school."

"He just needs time to have his little hissy fit. Guys like him just want what they can't have. I'm not saying he's like all the other born-rich guys around here—if he were, I wouldn't be friends with him."

"If you say so."

"Don't let him ruin our night." He leans over to kiss my cheek.

"I won't. I'm excited to see your parents' restaurant."

"They'll be really excited to meet you, so get ready."

I stop in my tracks again. *Shit. I didn't have time to put my undies back on. I cannot meet Chase's parents for the first time while I'm going commando.*

"Um. I need to grab a water at Starbucks real quick."

"Really? We're almost there."

"I'm just really thirsty."

"Okay. We're almost at the restaurant. Where they serve beverages."

I squeeze my eyes shut and wrinkle my nose. "I have to put my underwear back on."

He lowers his head, smiling. "Right this way." He holds the Starbucks door open for me. "Efficient, excellent time management skills, and she knows how to make a good first impression with the parents. You're the best."

"You are," I say. And he is.

———

I'm not in the habit of ranking hugs, but I am about ten seconds into one of the best hugs of my life. Maybe *the* best. Perhaps it's because she's a chef, but Chase's mom makes a meal out of her hugs. I feel like crying.

"So nice to meet you, *bella.*"

"I'm so happy to meet you!"

She finally pulls back to look at me and touch my face. "These eyes! Look at those eyes!"

"I can't stop looking at them," Chase says.

His mother is beautiful, all soft curves and warm smiles. "Aww, he's so in love, listen to him." She turns to Chase and smacks him on the arm. "Why you not tell us you're coming, huh?! I coulda fixed something special."

"I'm gonna fix something special for her tonight. Looks like you're busy."

The restaurant is at least three-quarters full, inside and out.

"Ohh, you gonna cook for her?" She nudges me. "Lucky girl. He only cooks for the special people."

"Who's this?!" The booming voice comes from a handsome man who looks exactly like I hope Chase will look in about thirty years, but with different hair. He punches Chase's arm. "Don't tell me. Don't tell me this is 'girl trouble?'"

"Aimee, this is my dad, Sean McKay."

"So nice to meet you, sir."

Sean McKay's handshake is the equivalent of Graziella's hug—warm and robust. "Don't you 'sir' me, woman. What's a fine thing like you doing with a manky gobshite like this?" He musses up his son's hair, clearly a fan of his. "What can I get for ya to drink? Lemme guess. Moscow Mule."

Chase's eyes meet mine and we laugh. "I'll have whatever Chase is having."

"Whiskey it is, then. She's a keeper."

"Tell me about it," Chase replies. He leads me to the kitchen.

"I see you back there in a minute," his mother says, patting me on the back as she stops to chat with customers.

Chase is greeted by everyone in the kitchen like a beloved king who's returned from battle. He's really in his element here, although he seems to be in his element everywhere.

"Everyone, this is Aimee Gilpin, my girlfriend. Aimee, this is everyone."

I wave to everyone.

"Hope you like spaghetti alla bolognese. It's off-menu but I prefer it to the fettucine."

"Hey!" says one of the line cooks. "Cover your hair in here, you animal!"

Chase grabs a hairnet from a dispenser and puts it on while filling up a pot with water. "Have a seat over there, *bella*," he says, winking at me.

Dio mio! It's a good thing I'm wearing panties, because that wink would have caused me to leave a wet spot on this stool.

Not many people on this earth can make a hairnet look hot, but Chase McKay is doing it.

In every way, he just does it for me.

From the people who made him, to the spaghetti alla bolognese he's making for me—for the first time since I moved to New York, I feel like I'm at home.

CHAPTER 24
CHASE

TWO MONTHS LATER

When the chauffeur double-parks outside Aimee's apartment building, I let him know that I can open the door to let myself out. I've been riding up front with him since he picked me up a few minutes ago. I made the decision to hire a BMW car service instead of Uber to take us to Greg Lee's wedding at The Plaza, since this is our first formal date, but I would rather take the bus in my tux than sit alone in the backseat. No matter how rich I get. And I will get very rich.

I texted Aimee a minute ago, to let her know we were almost there. I had every intention of going up to her apartment to fetch her, but she steps out onto the sidewalk before I'm even at the door. Ever the efficient and timely professional, she is a fucking knockout in a deep blue floor length gown that matches her eyes and makes me want to drop to my knees. The neckline is pretty respectable, but it will have other men drooling, nonetheless. She kisses my cheek then gives me a little twirl. That exposed back will have my hand on it all night.

"You're stunning."

She steps back, slides the dark sunglasses down the bridge of her nose and whistles as she checks me out in my tuxedo. "You are not so bad yourself, Sexy McSexy-pants." She scrunches up her face. "Forget I just said that or pretend I said something really cool instead."

"Done."

She runs her fingers through my hair. "I'm glad you left your hair down."

The driver holds the back door open for Aimee, and I hurry around to the street side to get in next to her. As soon as we're both settled into the backseat, we're holding hands and kissing like we're on our way to prom. It's been like this for two months. I can't remember the last time she wore lipstick when I was around. And I'm around her almost every night.

"Keaton's going to be there with Quinn, right?" she asks.

"Far as I know."

She nods and looks out the darkened window.

Things with Keaton have been mostly back to normal as far as I'm concerned, but this will be the first time the three of us have been together for almost two months. The last time she saw him, he left the office early on her last day at SnapLegal when we were having a little party for her. He wasn't being an asshole exactly, but he wasn't being a prince either. It helps that our revenue's already up ten percent since we transitioned to subscription. Since he respects revenue and he associates Aimee with the transition, he's only had good things to say about her.

But I can tell she's nervous about seeing him socially, so it's my job to take her mind off of it. As we merge onto the Brooklyn Bridge to head over the East River to Manhattan, I ask her if she knows about the history of it. She laughs and shakes her head.

"Tell me," she says. "I love your history lessons."

"This was the first suspension bridge to use steel for its cable wires. It took fourteen years to build, around the end of the 19th Century. John Augustus Roebling initially designed it—he was from Germany. He was injured when he was surveying the East River, and eventually he died from a tetanus infection, and that left his son Washington Roebling in charge of construction.

Not long after construction began, Washington got the bends—you know, compression sickness. It left him incapacitated, so his wife Emily took over. Washington had to stay inside their apartment in Brooklyn and he'd watch through field glasses and then send written messages down to the site through her, but she studied mathematics and figured out all of the engineering intricacies involved. Nearly thirty people died in the construction of this bridge."

"This is impressive, but not quite as touching as the Wonder Wheel story."

I'm realizing now that all of the historical anecdotes I tell her involve husbands and wives, for some reason …

"Anyway. Emily Warren Roebling was the first person to cross the Brooklyn Bridge. She carried a rooster. As a symbol of victory. A week later, people were concerned that the bridge would collapse, so they let PT Barnum parade twenty-one elephants across it. Nobody had any doubts after that."

I pull her hand onto my lap.

"That day that Keaton told me about you turning him down when he went to your place at lunch, I had to get out of the office. I just started walking, and I walked across this bridge, both ways. Trying to keep moving, trying to decide what to do."

"Oh God, you weren't thinking of jumping, were you?!"

"Naw. I wouldn't do that to my parents. But I almost hurled my phone into the river to keep from calling you."

She smiles and kisses me. "I'm so glad I found you at the bar. I love you."

"I love you too."

I had my reasons for staying away from her then, but I'll never have any doubts about us now.

Love is a river, but a relationship is a bridge, connecting two very different living things that belong together. Engineered and built with blood, sweat, and tears, across this fluid entity with unexpected depths, which flows in different directions at different times. It can be a pain in the ass to deal with, depending on the time of day or day of the week, but it's always worth it once you get to where you want to be. And I want to be with Aimee. But I won't give up on Keaton Bridges.

CHAPTER 25
AIMEE

Greg Lee's wedding is by far the fanciest and most formal nuptial event I have ever experienced. I have never seen two people with such perfect glowing skin marry each other before. It's my first time at the storied Plaza Hotel, in the Grand Ballroom. And it's the first time I get to see my boyfriend in a tuxedo. He is so devastatingly handsome and sexy I feel exhilarated every time I look at him.

I am not the only female at this table who can't take her eyes off of him either.

Keaton's lovely, waif-like and somewhat inanimate socialite girlfriend Quinn has basically been eye-fucking him ever since we were introduced to her.

This has not gone unnoticed by Keaton.

I don't care how many times Chase has told me that Keaton's a good guy and a good friend and a good investor. As far as I'm concerned, he's an insecure asshole who's jealous of everything that Chase has and everything that Chase is, and he's nowhere near man enough to admit it. I'm surprised he's never snuck into Chase's room and shaved off his beautiful hair while he was sleeping.

But honestly, Chase has been holding back so much resentment about Keaton too, and I'm getting pretty tired of being a witness to their dynamic. I may be the reason that things are coming to a head for them now, but I am just the tip of the iceberg … The tipsy tip. I may have had more to drink than I should have.

Once the alcohol started flowing, so did the acerbic barbs between Keaton and Chase, just like that time we all rode the elevator after I rode Chase in his office.

"When people see us together, they assume he's my drug dealer, not my CEO," Keaton jokes when someone at the table is surprised that Chase is a CEO of his own company at twenty-seven.

"And they assume you're just hanging out with me to make yourself look cooler—and they're right."

There's polite but awkward laughter, but the only thing that's stopping me from giving Keaton a piece of my mind are the pieces of cake and sips of champagne that keep my mouth occupied. That and Chase's hand, which is almost always stroking my bare back. His thumb brushes my skin, fingertips lazily caressing me while he chats with the man sitting next to him. Even when he's sparring with Keaton, he's able to subtly soothe me with his touch.

And yet, I still want to knee Keaton in the balls.

"So … Tracy, is it?" Quinn asks while twirling strands of silky blonde hair around her index finger and eyeing Chase.

"Aimee."

"Right. How did you and Chase meet?"

She leans toward me and away from Keaton, but he can hear us. He makes a point of watching me while I answer.

"Oh, you know. We met at a bar, and then we ended up working together for a while. Not much of a story." I shrug, and glance over at Keaton.

He's got that poker face again. He blinks slowly, then angles away from Quinn to strike up a conversation with the person next to him. I suppose he's decided that it's safe to let us girl-talk with each other.

"How did you and Keaton meet?" I ask her.

"Oh, it's such a cute story," she says. "We met at a mutual friend's birthday party at Cipriani."

I wait for her to continue to the cute part of the story, but I guess that was it.

"Cipriani downtown," she elaborates. "Not 42nd Street."

"Awww. Cute!"

"I know, right?" She leans in even closer and lowers her voice. "It's interesting, though ... From the way Keaton always talks about Chase, I thought they were really good friends. But they act more like ..."

"Yeah. I know what you mean. I think it's just a phase or something."

"Maybe," she says, tilting her head as she looks over at Keaton. "I think Keaton's just jealous."

Well, maybe you're not as vacuous as you seem, Miss Parker.

"What's that, babe?" Keaton raises his chin at her. "You think I'm just what?"

Quinn ignores him and rolls her eyes at me. They are really good at posing for pictures together, but something tells me all is not well in their world.

Fortunately, the deejay announces that it's time for us to welcome the bride and groom to the dance floor, and everyone's attention turns to Greg and his gorgeous wife. They do a choreographed routine to a mash up that begins with "Let's Stay Together," transitions to "SexyBack" and ends with "Crazy in Love" and the married couple waving guests onto the dance floor to come join them.

I don't picture Chase as the dancing type, so I don't bother suggesting that we get out there, but he pushes his chair back, stands up and holds his hand out to pull me up.

If someone had told me three months ago that one day I'd be dancing with Chase McKay to a Beyoncé song in a ballroom, I would have laughed in their hilarious insane face while secretly praying that it would happen.

Well, it's happening, and I guess it shouldn't surprise me that the man's got moves. He isn't showy, and he doesn't expend a lot of energy or take up a lot of space, but he's dancing to turn me on and make me laugh. Mission. Accomplished. I grab his face and kiss him—mindful not to let myself get carried away as usual, because this is a family affair. As soon as I've let go of him, the mother of the groom dances over to say "hello" to Chase. He takes her hand, gives her a twirl, and leaves her fanning herself as she goes back to join her son. Greg jokingly shakes his fist at him and yells, "hands off my mom!"

This is an awesome party, but I wonder how much longer we have to stay here.

I'm about to ask Chase if we should look into getting a room, when Quinn drags Keaton over. It's a mistake, because contrary to what Chase said, Keaton looks much *less* cool next to him. Quinn obviously agrees with me, because she starts swaying her hips and rolling her shoulders just a little too close to Chase.

Chase takes both of my hands, and I watch Keaton's face. Not only does he not look cool, he looks like he's boiling over.

When Quinn rubs her shoulder against Chase's arm, Keaton blurts out, "Okay that's it!"

As if Chase is the one behaving inappropriately, Keaton steps up to him. "You wanna have a word with me in the men's room, *friend?*"

"Yeah I think it's about time we had words, *friend.*" Chase lets go of my hands, kisses my cheek and tells me he'll be right back.

And then he storms off the dance floor, with Keaton.

That's when I realize, through a thin bubbly haze, that no matter how much I love him, the story of Aimee and Chase will always be the story of Aimee and Chase and Keaton.

Or …

Or is this all the story of Chase and Keaton and I'm just a guest star?

Quinn seems amused by the drama, smiling with her eyes and mouth wide open as she watches them go.

Tyler from the sales department moonwalks over to me and starts dancing around.

I can't do this. I signal for him to dance with Quinn, which he is more than happy to do. I tell Quinn that I have to go out to make a phone call, but I don't think she hears me.

I return to the table to get my purse. I need some air. I need to walk around, maybe try to find a store in Midtown that sells sage wands so I can cleanse the aura of this table.

I'll send Chase a text to let him know where I am.

I have every intention of coming back when I feel better.

I just don't know when that will be.

CHAPTER 26
CHASE

Every step I take from the dance floor amps up a decade's worth of unresolved tension between me and Keaton. My dad was right. We need to kick each other in the balls.

As soon as we're inside the men's room, Keaton takes a swing at me, and since I'm ready for it I lean in.

I'm giving you this one, you fucking pussy.

It's a blow, but it doesn't hurt much. It just unleashes everything. He's so surprised that he actually hit me, I take the opportunity to come at him hard with a punch to the chin that knocks him backwards.

"You fucking dick!" he yells, rubbing his jaw. "You hit me!"

"You hit me first, you lazy fucking trust fund baby!"

He charges at me, trying to tackle me like a linebacker, but I use his momentum to knee him in the gut.

"You piece of shit," he says, through clenched teeth. "You need to think I'm lazy, don't you? If it weren't for me, you never would have gotten funded for as much as you did right out of the gate!"

He shoves my chest and I almost lose my balance.

Wrong.

Delusional.

Prick.

"If it weren't for me, you wouldn't be a CFO. Nobody else would have given you that title!"

He swipes at me again, but I lean back and he misses my face by a mile. I shove him back into the wall. He sneers at me.

"You only started this company because you knew nobody would ever hire you as a lawyer—except maybe a biker gang."

He comes at me again, trying to tackle me again. I wrap my arms around his torso, binding his arms so he can't do anything.

"I bet you love that people think you're jealous of me!" he spits out.

"Actually, I'm too happy living my life to give a shit what people think—you should give it a try."

I let him go because it's just pathetic seeing him struggle like this.

He punches me in the stomach, and I punch him in the jaw again.

"Owwww! You fucking dick!" He cradles his jaw in his hand.

I stretch out my fingers and flick my wrist because that fucker's chiseled jawline is so fucking bony.

He takes a deep, pained breath. "I can't believe you fucked the girl I liked again."

"This is the only time it's happened. And grow the fuck up. Aimee never liked you that way."

"Oh yeah? You gonna go for Quinn now too?"

I give him a look. *As if.*

"I don't know what it is, but the rich girls just love the idea of slumming it with you, don't they?"

"Yeah, well. So do the rich guys, apparently."

I'm rubbing my stomach and he's rubbing his jaw and we both grin at each other. Neither of us went for the nose or the solar plexus, or any body parts that could really get damaged. It was a quick, fair fight.

"If you think I'm not loyal—fuck you. I walked away from Aimee out of loyalty to you and the company, but at some point it became more about her. If that pisses you off then there's nothing I can say or do to change that. We'll always have our differences, and if you decide you want out of the company, then *do* it. Just don't you fucking dare try to convince yourself that I'm not loyal to you. Moron."

I watch his expression change, and know that he's finally really heard me.

The door to the men's room opens and an elderly gentleman walks in, nods at us as he heads for one of the stalls.

Keaton and I go over to the sinks to wash our hands. When our eyes meet in the mirror, we both start laughing. We don't have to say anything—we both know we're thinking the same thing. *That felt so fucking good.*

"Dick" he says, under his breath.

"Fuck you," I whisper.

"Thanks for not breaking my nose. You really are a

thoughtful guy."

"About time you figured that out. Idiot."

He runs his fingers through his hair, smiling, then stares down at his reddened knuckles. "I have a feeling I'll be breaking up with Quinn tonight."

I don't know what to say, other than: "You deserve better."

"Yeah. Tell that to Aimee."

I cock an eyebrow.

He pats me on the back.

"Kidding. You're a cute couple. You're a lucky guy. Maybe I am jealous." He holds the door open for me.

"Yeah." I pat him on the back. "I know."

When I get back to the table and don't find Aimee there, I scan the room looking for her.

"Have you guys seen my girlfriend?" I ask Tyler and Quinn.

Tyler shakes his head, vehemently. "No and I definitely did not ask her to dance."

Quinn says, "I think she had to go outside to make a phone call."

That's when I notice that her purse isn't there. I check my phone for a message from her, but there isn't one. When Keaton gets back to the table and finds Tyler with Quinn, he buttons up his jacket and walks off to chat up a bridesmaid. When he decides to move on, he moves on.

I expect to find Aimee in the foyer, but she's not there. I think for sure I'll find her in the lobby, but she's not there either. I walk out to the front entrance of the hotel—no sign of Aimee anywhere.

I call her phone, which goes to voicemail after four rings. I send her a text with a bunch of question marks.

It's so unlike her to disappear like this.

I go back to wait around outside the ladies' room, checking my phone for a reply that never comes.

I wonder if she somehow saw or heard me and Keaton fighting and it pissed her off.

Would it piss her off?

Yeah. It would.

I'm an asshole. I shouldn't have left her to go off with him. I don't blame her if she's mad at me.

I call her again, leaving a message this time.

I try her business cell phone, just for the hell of it, but that goes straight to voicemail.

After doing one full tour around the ballroom without finding Aimee, I decide to call Tim the driver to have him bring the car up front.

By the time he's picked me up, I've called her phone three more times. I don't even know if she knows her way around Midtown. Maybe she just got a car home.

Five minutes after telling the driver to take me back to Aimee's place, I get a call from Aimee's phone.

"Thank fuck—where are you?"

"Chase?" It's not Aimee's voice. "It's Roxy. She left her phone in the bathroom. Why do you keep calling— isn't she with you?"

Shit.

I tell Roxy to tell Aimee to call me as soon as she gets home, if she gets home, but that I'm going back to my place to see if she went there since our plan was to stay at my place tonight.

Fucking Keaton.

It's as much my fault as his that I keep letting him get between me and Aimee.

I punch the passenger door.

"We'll find her, Mr. McKay," the driver says. "I got all night. I'll take you wherever you need to go."

"Thanks, man." I massage my aching hand. "It just might take all night."

I've felt a little sick to my stomach ever since I got the call from Roxy, but once we get to my place and Aimee isn't there, I feel a level of panic that I've never really felt before. What if I've not only lost Aimee, but I actually *lost* Aimee? What if something's happened to her?

I have Tim drop me off at Bitters, thinking maybe she figured it would be poetic for us to find each other there again, but she's nowhere to be found.

Again, I call Roxy to see if Aimee's showed up. She hasn't heard from her.

When Tim asks me if there's anywhere else that I want to go, I look out into the street and see a couple making out in the back of a cab, and it hits me.

If she decided to go anywhere besides home, and there's still any hope of us being together, there is one other place she would go. Now, instead of feeling panicky in my gut, I'm excited. I know where she is. I'm going to find her.

"Yeah," I say. "There is."

CHAPTER 27
AIMEE

I can't believe I'm here without Chase. I can't believe I'm here, wandering around in my sleeveless flowing evening gown and heels, with a champagne buzz, arms wrapped around myself like I'm doing a re-make of Avril Lavigne's "I'm With You" video.

Fortunately, it is not "a damn cold night." It's a warm and humid summer night. Once I'd left the hotel and realized that I didn't bring my phone with me, I just walked around, huffing and puffing. When I saw the entrance to the subway station I stood in front of the steps, trying to decide if I should go back now, but a bunch of people were trying to get around me. Being the Midwestern girl that I am, I apologized for standing in their way and followed the flow of the crowd down into the station.

I'll just get on the first train that comes, I thought to myself. *I'll get off at the next stop.*

The first train that came was the Q, and when I realized it would take me all the way back to Brooklyn, I figured I should just go home and find my phone so I could call Chase. But then I thought about how he didn't have his phone on him that Sunday night when I was trying to get in touch with him about my new job.

My God, it feels like so long ago.

I started replaying that whole night in my mildly inebriated mind, and before I knew it, I had missed my stop and the train was in Coney Island.

My first stop at Luna Park was the Cyclone. Somehow it felt safer to be standing in line by myself and riding an old roller coaster on my own than walking around the amusement park. But it's such a nice night, and it's so crowded, I'm sure there's really no reason to be nervous about being alone.

I make my way to the Zoltar machine. I certainly did ride the winds of change, he was right about that. At times, things did seem to be out of touch. Like right now, for instance. I find a dollar bill in my purse, smooth it out and feed it into the machine. The creepy animatronic fortune teller blinks and comes to life. He says the same thing he said the last time. "You must live each day as if it is your last …" Sure, Zoltar. Doin' it.

I retrieve the small yellow card from the dispenser and hold it up to the neon lights so I can read it.

A new turn of events will soon come about. A happy reunion with a loved one will make life all that you ever wanted it or dreamed it to be …

Well. Wouldn't that be nice.

I look around, spotting no one that I recognize, no wavy hair bobbing up and down through the crowds.

It's stupid to stay here. I should just go home.

Looking up at the Wonder Wheel, I remember the story that Chase told me about Deno and his wife, and the sweet young couple that had gotten engaged while we were on it. I wonder if that couple is married already, if they're still together. I'm sure they are.

I decide to ride the Wonder Wheel by myself, just once before I go.

Okay, that was a terrible idea.

Riding the roller coaster while tipsy was somehow less nauseating, possibly because it was constant motion. Sitting alone in one of those cars while it rolled and swayed back and forth mid-air was just horrifying. I didn't puke, but I felt so stupid. Even with the beautiful view, all I could think about was how it just felt wrong to be here without Chase. I think it would feel wrong to be anywhere without Chase. It doesn't matter how we got to the place of being together, or who else is around, all that matters to me is that I'm with him. I'll take it all, including the questionable best friend. The bitter and the sweet and all of the surprising, unexpected flavor combinations that I have never experienced before.

I cannot climb out of that hell car fast enough. My legs are wobbly, my brain is wobbly, but I am determined to get home so I can call Chase. I nearly trip while I'm rushing out the exit, so I slow down and watch the ground in front of my feet. That doesn't help at all because I smash right into someone.

"Sorry!" I say, without looking up.

A man's hands grip my arms, and as soon as he touches me, I feel drunk again.

"Don't be," he says.

I throw my arms around his neck. "You're here. I can't believe you found me." He would totally find me and rescue me if there's ever a zombie apocalypse.

"I *thought* I heard you screaming."

"I'm sorry I left you."

"I'm sorry I left you, but don't ever walk around New York without a phone again."

I kiss him all over his face. I run my fingers through his glorious hair. He kisses me so hard and holds me so tight that I can barely breathe. It's all Chase's lips and spinning neon lights and guys hooting and hollering around us. We are twenty-seven and reckless and in love and together.

"Aimee," he says, so serious that I worry something's wrong.

"What? What's wrong?"

"Nothing's wrong." He kisses my forehead. "Listen to me." He kisses my cheekbone. "You're my best friend now. I love you. You've become the most important thing in my life. I didn't plan for this, so I don't have a ring for you yet, but I want you to know that I want to marry you. I've known it deep down ever since the first time we were standing here. I've known it since the second I saw you. I want you. You're mine."

"Yes. You're mine."

"Yes."

"I want to marry you too … Wait. Are you proposing to me?"

"Yes." He laughs. "Are you accepting my proposal?"

I smile and raise both hands in the air, jumping up and down and screaming like that girl from a few months ago. "We're engaged! We just got engaged!"

He covers his face, shaking his head. "You're drunk."

"Yes. I am. On you. And you're gonna marry me!"

"Eventually, yes."

My lips smash into his again.

What a night.

We are twenty-seven and reckless and in love and reunited by the Wonder Wheel, and the only thing stopping me from dry humping Chase McKay in the middle of Luna Park is knowing that I'll be able to come home to him every day and every night for the rest of my life.

EPILOGUE

EVERY DAY, EVERY NIGHT

CHASE

TWO YEARS LATER

W e've been to a lot of weddings together since Greg Lee's, and all of them were a more pleasant experience for us than that one. But this one takes the cake. And by cake, I mean the massive Italian wedding cake that my mom made. This is the best cake I've ever had, and the best wedding I've ever been to, because this one is ours. This is the wedding of Aimee Lynn Gilpin to Chase Luca McKay.

While I can easily afford to pay for this whole event, once word got out to our clients half a year ago that we'd finally picked a date, so many local businesses volunteered their services and gifted us their products

—from the flower arrangements to the venue. This huge loft in Greenpoint is perfect, with the view of the river and beyond, but what really does it for me is the hanging strings of warm white lights. They've always made me want to feel in love, and I do. Every day, every night, ever since I met my wife.

She looks so beautiful in her wedding dress—truly glowing and giddy despite her inability to drink the champagne or the Irish whiskey.

Roxy is wrapping up her maid of honor speech, which has been paused three times by Aimee getting up to hug her. Turns out Foxy Roxy is a total cheeseball beneath the surface. That's not surprising to me, given who her best friend is.

Now it's time for the best man to take over the microphone. Aimee rubs my thigh and gives Keaton a hoot and holler. That they have become friends in the past couple of years is something that did surprise me, and it moves me that my two best friends are good friends now too.

This woman. My wife. She still moves me, like nothing else can.

"Hey everyone, I'm Keaton Bridges." He clears his throat. I can tell he's getting choked-up already. "It's an honor for me to have the title of best man tonight, but Chase McKay is the best man that I know. A little over two years ago, I showed up at a bar one night, late for meeting my best friend, after begging him to come out for a drink with me. I made a bee-line for this beautiful woman that was standing next to him and bought her a drink, because that's what I do. Chase went back to the office to work, because that's what he does. Little did I know, he had spent about half an hour falling for that beautiful woman before I showed up. But he saw how much I liked her, and he let me go for it. That's another thing that he does. He observes, he thinks, he makes quick smart decisions that he believes are best for everyone in the long-term, and he doesn't make a fuss. The beautiful woman was so nice and polite—it took her an entire month to get it through my thick skull that she wasn't interested in me. No accounting for taste I guess.

It took me another few months to figure out what Chase and Aimee knew from the moment they met—that they are perfect together. I've known Chase since we were in college, and he's always been the guy that everyone wanted to be around, the guy that made me a better person. But when he and Aimee are together, they become this metaphorical third thing that's better than anything I've ever witnessed. They've created an awesome new home together, a successful new company, and now ..." He pauses, to clear his throat again. I've never seen Keaton's eyes tear up before, but it's happening now, in front of two hundred and fifty people.

"Now they're creating an actual third person for all of us to love, and I want you both to know that I will do anything I can for you and your family, always." He looks down at me and gives me the grin that makes his face more recognizable. "You complete me. And she completes you. I love you, man."

He puts down the microphone, and I get up to hug him for maybe the second time in our lives.

"I love you too, man."

Aimee gets up to hug him, and he rubs her belly.

I look around the room, at my parents and grandparents, Aimee's parents and grandparents, our partners and co-workers and clients and friends from all over.

No matter how many bad choices we've made in our past, tonight there is good food, good music, good drinks, good people, and I get to enjoy it with the one person I've found who matters more to me than anyone else.

ACKNOWLEDGMENTS

Special thanks to Mackenzie Cartwright & Teddy Hamilton for lending their voices to the audiobook version and making my words funnier, sexier, sweeter and more romantic.

Printed in Great Britain
by Amazon

24722478R00138